Welcome t

Whirlwind
Weddings

WHIRLWIND WEDDINGS is a miniseries that
combines the heady romance of a whirlwind
courtship with the joy of a wedding. You'll enjoy
marriages made not so much in heaven as
in a hurry!

This month's book is a sensational debut in Harlequin
Romance® from the sizzling Temptation Blaze author,
Janelle Denison. **READY-MADE BRIDE** is a powerful
and passionate romance with a twist in its tail!

JANELLE DENISON writes: "I met my husband when I
was sixteen, and, if my parents had allowed it, I would
have married him within a week. However, we did the
practical thing and waited five years to tie the knot.
The ceremony was a girl's dream come true, the
groom the handsomest man in the church. The
reception was magical and fun, and, rascal that my
husband is, he had no qualms about taking my garter
off with his teeth! Over a decade of wonderful
memories, I still think back to that beautiful April day
with a dreamy smile, knowing I'd marry my husband
all over again—even in a quick, whirlwind wedding."

Dear Reader,

The world is made up of words, which most of us read and take for granted. After all, learning to read is taught to us at an early age. But how does someone who sacrificed their education to help support their family cope with not knowing how to read?

Ready-Made Bride is a story that touched my heart from the moment of its inception. So did the gruff hero, who harbored a shocking secret. I knew it would take a special heroine to reach him, a woman who believed in him when he'd long since stopped believing in himself. With the help of one mischievous little boy, these two lonely people learn what love is all about. And with love, *anything* is possible.

I hope you enjoy Kane and Megan's story as much as I loved writing it.

Happy reading!

Janelle Denison

What others have said about Janelle Denison:

"The inspirational and realistic portrayal of one man's struggle to learn to read and to love."
—Marsha L. Tait, President, **Literacy Volunteers of America, Inc.**

"Janelle Denison handles an emotional subject with skill and tenderness. Her wonderful debut for Harlequin Romance® will stir the heart as easily as it coaxes a smile."
—**Award-winning author Day Leclaire**

"Reading is fun and fundamental. So is love. *Ready-Made Bride* compellingly tells why."
—Roy Blatchford, U.K. Director, **Reading Is Fundamental, National Literacy Trust**

Of *Private Fantasies*, Harlequin Temptation®:
"Janelle Denison combines steamy sexual tension and intriguing characters to produce a scorching page-turner."
—*Romantic Times*

Ready-Made Bride
Janelle Denison

Whirlwind
Weddings

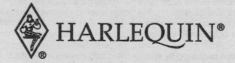

HARLEQUIN®

TORONTO • NEW YORK • LONDON
AMSTERDAM • PARIS • SYDNEY • HAMBURG
STOCKHOLM • ATHENS • TOKYO • MILAN • MADRID
PRAGUE • WARSAW • BUDAPEST • AUCKLAND

This book is dedicated to my brothers, Jay, Jeff and Kirk, heroes in their own right. And to the women who put up with them, Erin, Karen and Debbie, wonderful sisters and extraordinary heroines.
And, as always, to my husband, Don, who gives new meaning to the word *hero*. You continually amaze me with your patience, belief and love. This wonderful dream wouldn't be possible without your support and encouragement.

ISBN 0-373-03531-4

READY-MADE BRIDE

First North American Publication 1998.

Copyright © 1998 by Janelle R. Denison.

PROLOGUE

His dad needed a wife, and he wanted a mom. Seven-year-old Andrew Fielding had found the perfect woman for both of them.

Sitting at the oak desk his dad had made for him and chewing on the eraser end of his pencil, Andy reread the letter he'd written inviting Megan Sanders to come and visit his second grade class for his eighth birthday next month. They'd been penpals for over a year and a half, ever since he'd written to tell her how much he liked the books she wrote called *Andy's Adventures.*

They were great adventures. Just the kind he got into. And the boy in the pictures looked like him, too, with blond hair and brown eyes. Andrew liked to pretend he was Megan's Andy, fighting imaginary pirates and building fortresses to ward off Indians.

She wasn't married and didn't have any kids. She'd even written in one of her letters that she wished she had a little boy as wonderful as he was.

He wanted her for a mom, to take care of him and his dad and bake cookies on rainy days.

His dad needed a wife, to make him laugh and smile more often. Someone to convince him to make up with Grandpa and Grandma Linden.

Megan could do all that, and Andrew knew his dad would love her as much as he did.

It was the perfect plan.

Now all he had to do was get his dad to fall in love with her.

CHAPTER ONE

"DAD! She's coming, she's coming!" Andy bounded down the porch stairs just as Kane exited his pickup. He waved a piece of paper in his hand, his face wreathed in excitement. "She's coming for my birthday next month!"

Kane Fielding eyed his son curiously as they headed for the back door leading into the house. "*Who's* coming for your birthday?"

Andrew skipped next to his side. "Megan is!"

His brows rose in surprise and a little disbelief. "Megan Sanders? The woman who writes those books you read?"

"Yep!"

Kane knew who Megan was. How could he not when that's all his son ever talked about—Megan Sanders and the Andy's Adventures stories she wrote. Some days he regretted the day he'd walked into the bookstore in the city and had asked for a good children's book for his son, who was just starting to read. The clerk had told him that Andy's Adventures was the hottest series for young boys. The catchy title had amused Kane and enthralled his son enough to write the woman a fan letter that had evolved into a friendship.

"Care to tell me how this came about?" Kane asked, not certain he *really* wanted to know.

"I wrote her a letter and invited her to come and visit for my birthday." Andrew grinned at him, seeming pleased with himself. "And I told her she could stay with us and that you wouldn't mind."

Kane held open the screen door for Andrew, then followed him into the kitchen. Maintaining a long-distance friendship with the author was one thing, but to actually invite her to Linden? "Andrew, you don't even know her."

"Yes, I do, and you do, too." A frown creased Andrew's

6

forehead. "She calls all the time, and you've talked to her on the phone."

Kane set his lunch box on the counter, unable to refute Andrew's claim. After his and Megan's initial introduction, he only spoke to her briefly each time she called, just enough to let that soft voice of hers tie him inside out and make him wonder, for a second or two, what she was really like before he handed the phone over to Andrew. He'd never minded her talking to his son because Andrew received so much pleasure from their conversations.

"Talking to her on the phone and receiving letters from her isn't the same thing as really knowing her," Kane tried explaining.

The pure and simple joy in his son's eyes slowly died, and his shoulders slumped. "You don't want her to come visit?"

Kane scrubbed a hand over his jaw, hating the disappointment in Andrew's voice, and that he'd caused it. "No, it's not that—"

"Will you at least read the letter she wrote?" he asked, a hopeful catch to his voice.

Kane stared at the piece of paper Andrew extended toward him, then casually moved to the sink and turned on the tap. "Why don't you read it to me while I wash up?"

Kane listened to his son recite the letter, about Megan telling him she'd love to drive out and visit and stay with them as long as it was okay with his dad. Kane cringed. Great, she was leaving the decision up to him.

Once Andrew was done, he looked at Kane expectantly. "So, can she come, Dad, please?"

Wiping his hands on a dish towel, he released a long breath. "I don't think her staying with us is a good idea."

"Why not?"

He gave Andrew a pointed look. "Because it's not proper." He hadn't so much as dated since his wife, Cathy, had died, at least not anyone in town. He could just imagine what a field day the gossips would have if they discovered he had a woman staying with him, no matter how platonic the arrangement.

Tears welled in Andrew's eyes and his throat bobbed as he swallowed. "This is all I want for my birthday. I was gonna take her to school to meet all my friends. I told them she was coming, and if she doesn't, they're gonna think I was lying."

Kane's heart twisted. Andrew rarely asked for anything, and he hated denying him the one thing he wanted so badly. Pushing his fingers through his thick hair, he turned his head and glanced out the kitchen window. He knew people would talk and speculate, but it wouldn't be the first time he'd been under scrutiny. And when did he care what the small-minded people of Linden thought, anyway?

"Please, Dad?" Andrew whispered.

How could he say no? Making Andrew happy was his main concern. And if having Megan nearby meant so much to his son, he was willing to take a little heat to give him his wish. Megan was, after all, just a friend visiting. A purely normal occurrence, he told himself, just as long as she didn't expect him to entertain her.

"She can stay here," Kane said on an expelled rush of breath.

Andrew's eyes grew round with delight and he danced around excitedly. "Yippee! Come on, Dad, let's go call her!" He raced into the living room.

Kane followed at a more leisurely pace, wondering what, exactly, he'd gotten himself into.

Megan Sanders's heart faltered as she stared at the sight in front of her. A man, a *gorgeous* specimen of a man, stood in the center of the barn she'd just stepped into, his back to her. He wore a pair of faded jeans that hugged long, muscular legs and a faded blue T-shirt that shaped a well-defined chest and back. Black hair, dusted with wood shavings and too long for traditional standards, curled at the nape of his neck.

This had to be Kane Fielding, she thought, tamping the

sudden fluttering in her belly that had little to do with the nerves she'd been experiencing on her two-day drive to Linden.

Busy concentrating on his carpentry, he hadn't heard her pull up to the main house or enter the barn. Breathing in the scent of man, sawdust and linseed oil, she watched as he sanded a flat piece of wood, then slowly caressed the length with long, strong fingers. He turned to examine the oak in the light, giving her a glimpse of his sharp, defined features and a full, sensual mouth. He was, by far, the most blatantly sexy man she'd ever encountered.

Knowing she couldn't just stare at him forever, she cleared her throat. "Excuse me?"

He whirled around, piercing green eyes narrowing on her. She'd envisioned Andy's father to be a larger version of the blond-haired boy, not this...renegade.

"I'm sorry, I didn't mean to startle you," she said, willing her pulse to a normal cadence. "I just tried the main house, but no one answered the door."

He watched her walk fully into the barn and approach him, his expression darkening, turning cautious. His mouth was firm, unsmiling, and his brooding gaze raked over her. So much for a warm welcome, she thought apprehensively. Maybe she had the wrong house. Her smile faltered.

"Can I help you?" His voice was deep, smooth and rich, belying the chilling intensity of his eyes.

"I'm hoping you can." She offered a smile. "Are you Kane Fielding?"

"Yeah, I'm Kane Fielding." Laying the wood on a nearby makeshift table cluttered with tools, he faced her again. He rested his hands on his hips, his stance defensive. "What can I do for you?"

Ignoring his ominous frown, she took the three final steps that separated them and extended her hand. "I'm Megan Sanders."

Obvious relief relaxed his features but didn't erase the caution. "*You're* Megan Sanders? You look nothing like your publicity photo."

Tentatively, he grasped her outstretched hand, his long fingers wrapping around her slender hand. Heat radiated up her arm, and her heart thumped in her chest. The swift, irrational attraction knocked her for a loop but oddly felt right. She'd learned enough from Andy's letters and her brief conversations with his father to know she'd like Kane, but she never dreamed she'd have this instantaneous response to him. Like she'd known him for years instead of only a handful of minutes.

Crazy, but the feeling was undeniably there.

"It's amazing what a makeup artist can do with straight hair and ordinary features," she said in an attempt to lighten the mood. "It's nice to finally meet you."

Kane let go of her hand, thinking she was far prettier than the small, black-and-white glamor shot printed on the back flap of her books—the one Andrew showed him every time he received one of Megan's books.

Ordinary features? Hardly. She had thick, shoulder-length auburn hair a man could lose his hands in and big blue eyes full of sparkle and life. Wearing a minimum of makeup, she looked fresh and wholesome, not at all what he expected of a best-selling author. She was petite, but the distinctly feminine curves outlined beneath her simple lavender dress and those shapely legs more than made up for her lack of height.

His body tightened in a subtle but unmistakable way.

Irritated that she had the ability to affect him so strongly, he kept his tone curt. "I wasn't expecting you until later this evening." And his first thought upon seeing her had been that she was a new representative from Human Services, sent by his in-laws to check on his parenting abilities. It wouldn't be the first time someone dropped by unannounced.

She clasped her hands behind her back and smiled despite his brusque attitude. "Actually, I made better time than I anticipated, and I didn't expect to find anyone home."

Normally, no one would have been. He only worked half

days at the sawmill on Fridays. He was home by one and used the extra time to get chores done around the house and make any appointments needed for Andrew or himself. The schedule worked well and afforded him more time with his son.

When he didn't reply, she shifted on her feet and asked, "Is Andrew home from school?" An anxious quality tinged her voice.

"Not yet." He glanced at his wristwatch. "The bus should be here any time."

"I can't tell you how much it means to me to be able to spend some time with Andrew."

He regarded her a little disbelievingly. "You do this for all your fans?"

"Andrew is the first," she admitted. "When he told me all he wanted for his birthday was for me to visit, I couldn't bring myself to disappoint him."

The kind gesture astounded him. "Why *my* son?"

Her expression softened, as did the incredibly blue hue of her eyes. "I care for Andrew very much."

"You hardly know him," he said, more gruffly than he intended.

"You'd be surprised how much I know. We've corresponded for a year and a half. Surely you must have read the letters he's written telling me about himself, and you."

If he answered her question honestly, she'd think he didn't care about his son. But the truth was far more complicated than a simple yes or no.

Tightening his jaw, he began putting away the tools scattered on the table. With a snap of his wrist, he tossed a tarp over the half-finished bookcase he was making for Andrew's birthday. "Why don't we go up to the house and you can wait for Andrew where it's cool?" *And I can figure out what I'm going to do about this mess I've made of things and what I'm going to do about you.*

He passed her, and she followed him outside into the sunshine and fresh air and up to the house. Entering from the front door, they walked through a small living room and into the kitchen.

He headed for the refrigerator. "Would you like something to drink? I have apple juice or beer."

"Apple juice sounds good," she said, sitting in one of the wooden chairs at the table.

He filled a glass with the cool liquid and set it on the table in front of her. Returning to the beer he'd left on the counter for himself, he took a long swig.

"How long do you plan on staying here in Linden?" he asked.

Her eyes met his. "At least a week, if it's not a problem."

His gaze strayed to the way she absently chewed on her bottom lip. He wondered if her mouth would taste as sweet and soft as it looked. Hell, a week would feel like a year.

He took another drink of beer, hoping it would douse the slow burn traveling through his veins. It didn't. "You have that kind of free time?"

"One of the perks of being a freelance writer." She grinned, her eyes dancing with humor. "You make your own hours and you don't have to answer to anyone except yourself, and on occasion, your editor." She took a drink of her juice. "So, do you mind?"

He blinked. "Do I mind what?"

"If I stay for a week." She rubbed her finger down the condensation gathering on her glass.

Yeah, he was beginning to mind a whole lot. What in the hell had be been thinking to tell Andrew that this woman, or any woman, for God's sake, could stay with them? And for an entire week?

"Linden is hardly a tourist town," he said, thinking to dissuade her. "There's not much here to keep you busy for a couple of days, let alone a week."

"I'm not really interested in touring the town," she replied, easily thwarting his plan. "I'm here to spend time with Andrew, if you don't mind my staying here, that is."

Realizing a woman like Megan was probably used to

more luxurious accommodations than what he had to offer, he said, "The house is small and nothing fancy."

He lived a simple life with Andrew, and he wouldn't apologize for the small house he'd inherited when his father had died. He'd been all of seventeen then, his younger sister, Diane, twelve, and he'd made this house the best home he could for the both of them. Except it hadn't been good enough for his wife. Nothing had been good enough for Cathy Linden after she'd learned the truth he'd kept hidden for most of his adult life.

Her mouth quirked. "I don't need anything out of the ordinary. A couch to sleep on will be fine." She stood, took her glass to the sink, then stopped in front of him. "I was hoping you'd let me do the cooking while I'm here, sort of a thank-you for letting me stay here."

A light feminine fragrance teased his senses and tightened his gut. "That's not necessary. In fact, I think—"

"I insist," she said, cutting him off before he could finish telling her that staying in his home wouldn't be such a good idea. "Besides, Andrew mentioned you're not real fond of cooking."

He set his empty beer bottle on the counter, feeling frustrated and edgy. "Andrew talks too much," he grumbled. Pulling in a deep breath, he met her wide, guileless gaze and tried again. "Megan, about staying here—"

The rumbling noise of a bus in the distance, then the squeal of brakes drifted from outside, stealing Megan's attention. She glanced toward the kitchen window, her eyes bright with expectation. "Is that Andrew?"

He mentally swore at the timely interruption. "It should be."

Her breath seemed to catch, and her eyes sparkled with excitement. "I want to go meet him."

And then she was gone, on her way through the living room and out the front door, leaving him standing alone in the kitchen, cursing fate and his son's bright idea...and that he'd stupidly agreed to it.

A minute later he stepped outside and onto the front

lawn. He stopped next to where Megan was waiting as Andrew hopped down the bus steps. Slinging his backpack over his shoulder, he started their way. His steps slowed when he saw the two of them, his gaze darting from Kane to Megan.

A dazzling smile curved her mouth. "There he is," she whispered, her voice catching on nervous laughter.

"Megan!" Andy's shout pierced the air, causing a flock of birds nestling in a nearby tree to scatter. He ran toward her, his short legs pumping as fast as they could. He flung himself against her, nearly knocking her off balance, and wrapped his arms tight around her waist. "You're really here!" he said, his shrill voice muffled against her breasts.

She returned the hug, her eyes shimmering with a rush of tears. "Of course I'm here, silly." She ruffled her fingers through his blond hair. "I told you I would be."

Andy untangled himself from her arms and looked at her. A sudden frown stole his bright smile. "Why are you crying, Megan?"

"Because I'm happy," she said, and gave a small sniffle. She cupped his chin in her palm, her adoration for him obvious. "You're even more handsome than the school picture you sent me."

Andy beamed. "And you're beautiful." He glanced at Kane, expectation and joy shining on his youthful face. "Don't you think Megan's beautiful, Dad?"

Don't drag me into the middle of this, son. He met her gaze, watching as a flush stole over her cheeks, enhancing the simple beauty in question. "Yeah, she's beautiful," he admitted.

She ducked her head and looked away, but not before he'd seen the pleasure lighting her eyes. The sun haloed her bent head, threading gold through the strands. Cinnamon fire, he thought, wondering if her hair felt as warm and silky as it looked.

They started toward the house, and Andy shifted his Power Ranger backpack to the other shoulder. "How long have you been here?" he asked, squinting at her.

"Not long at all," she replied, smoothing a hand lightly over the crown of his head, the gesture affectionate and maternal. "Just enough time for your father and I to get acquainted."

"Yeah?" Andy's gaze bounced from Megan to Kane, then back again. "So, do you guys like each other?"

"We like each other just fine, son," Kane interjected smoothly.

"I knew you would." An impish grin creased the dimple in Andrew's right cheek. Grabbing Megan's hand, he pulled her up the porch stairs. "Come on, Megan, I want to show you my room and where I keep all your books."

And in that moment, as he watched the pure joy on his son's face, Kane knew he'd lost the opportunity to send Megan away.

At the threshold, she stopped and glanced over her shoulder at Kane. The enchanting smile she gave him heated his temperature ten degrees and made him question his sanity for allowing her to stay with them for a week.

"Thank you, Kane," she said softly. Before he could reply she was whisked away by his impatient son.

He stood on the porch, knowing her gratitude was for letting her spend time with Andrew, but he couldn't help but feel like she was thanking him for something more.

Releasing a caustic laugh, he strode down the stairs and toward his workshop. "Who are you kidding, Kane?" he murmured to himself. "What would a woman like her see in a simple country boy like yourself?"

Old, buried bitterness scratched its way to the surface, and he quickly shoved it down. One woman had hated him for his insufficiencies. He wouldn't let another get that close, no matter how tempting she might be.

"Look at what my dad made me," Andy said, showing Megan the novelty wooden bookends on his dresser bracing a row of books. He fingered the intricately carved and brightly painted locomotive. "The front and back end of a train. Cool, huh?"

"Yes, they are." She eyed Kane's handiwork, impressed with his creative flair. She'd seen a brief glimpse of his talent in the barn, but hadn't realized the extent of his ability until now.

"I put all of my Andy's Adventures here, cuz they're special." He adjusted a hardbound volume that stuck out an inch farther than the rest before bending to open the last dresser drawer. "All my other books are in here. I don't have any other room for them."

She glanced into the open drawer, crammed with books of all sizes and variety. "You must love to read."

"Yep. Dad likes me to read, too." He pushed the drawer shut. "He's always bringing me books from the big bookstore in the city, but yours are my favorite."

"I'm glad." She sat on his bed and reclined on one forearm, discovering a simple pleasure in watching Andy's enthusiastic energy. She smiled, unable to recall the last time she'd done something just for herself, even something as simple as a vacation. Something spontaneous and adventurous and wonderfully reckless…like driving to Linden to meet the father and son who'd consumed so much of her thoughts over the past year and a half.

"And look at this," he went on, moving to a corner of the room. Straddling a wooden seat shaped like a real saddle, he secured his sneakered feet into lifelike stirrups, pulled back on leather reins and rocked. The smooth, perfectly sloped rockers moved soundlessly on the wooden floor. "He made me this rocking horse a couple of years ago for Christmas."

The rocker was like nothing she'd ever seen in any store, a one-of-a-kind original. "It's almost as big as you are."

"Yep." He flicked the reins, tousling the dark brown braided rope that made up the horse's mane. "Dad said he wanted to be sure I didn't outgrow it too fast. Did I ever tell you about the fort and swings he made for my school?"

"No." But she had a feeling he was going to tell her every little detail.

Smiling contentedly, she listened as Andrew continued

to rave about his father's virtues. Andrew's incessant chatter sounded like music to her hungry soul, filling up every empty, aching place in her. He made her forget for a brief time that the dreams she'd cultivated while growing up in various foster homes had been shattered by a husband more interested in climbing the corporate ladder than giving her the family they'd talked about. Somewhere along the way having children dropped to the bottom of his list of priorities.

After her divorce three years ago she'd immersed herself in her writing. She'd created a children's series, which had helped to fill the emptiness. She'd thought Andy's Adventures, and the precocious little boy she'd created had been fulfilling enough until Andrew Fielding had written her a fan letter and completely changed her life, giving her writing a new direction.

"Megan, you okay?"

A small, warm hand curled around her arm, and she glanced into his concerned face. Immediately, she sat up, hating that she'd somehow worried him. "I'm fine, why?

"Because you looked so sad."

She smiled for him and made up an excuse. "I was just thinking that I promised your father I'd make dinner. Maybe we should go see what we should have tonight."

Andy agreed, giving her a spontaneous hug that nearly unraveled her. "We're gonna have so much fun together, Megan."

She smiled into his baby soft hair. The week was going to fly by. "I'm planning on it."

He pulled back, eyes wide and brimming with anticipation. "Do you think we can bake chocolate chip cookies while you're here? They're my favorite, and Dad's, too."

Arching a brow, she stood. "He bakes cookies?"

Andy clasped her hand as they headed toward the kitchen. "Naw, he buys the hard kind from the grocery store, but he likes the soft, homemade ones I sometimes sneak home from Grandma's."

She nodded in understanding. "Then homemade chocolate chip cookies it will be."

"Yes!" he said zealously, and Megan wondered about
the mischievous sparkle in his eyes.

Andy shoveled a forkful of mashed potatoes into his mouth
and washed it down with a big gulp of milk that left a thin
mustache on his upper lip. "You're the best cook we ever
had, Megan," he said, wiping his mouth with his napkin.

"She's the only cook we've ever had, son," Kane interjected, before Megan took Andy's comment the wrong way
and thought he had a steady stream of women traipsing
through his house.

Andy shrugged and continued to eat like he hadn't been
fed in a week.

Kane's gaze shifted, meeting Megan's across the table.
Reluctantly, he agreed with Andy's assessment of Megan's
culinary skills. He hadn't been grocery shopping in almost
a week, yet she'd managed to make a hearty meal any man
would appreciate. She'd taken frozen, boneless chicken
breasts, thawed them in his microwave—which he hadn't
even known the contraption was capable of doing—then
she'd breaded the poultry and fried it in oil and herbs until
the outside was brown and crispy and the meat tender and
juicy.

"Aren't these mashed potatoes great, Dad?" Andy
asked, spooning a second serving onto his plate.

Kane frowned. "They aren't much different from the
ones I make." Except her mashed potatoes didn't have
lumps, and they tasted buttery, unlike his bland, pastelike
spuds.

"Megan adds butter and milk," Andy told him.

"A family secret?" he asked wryly, feeling a prick of
annoyance over his son's obvious heroine worship. Okay,
so he wasn't the best chef, but it wasn't as though they'd
starved before Megan's cooking.

"More like Betty Crocker's secret."

He stopped dragging a piece of chicken through the best gravy he'd ever tasted. "Pardon?"

"Betty Crocker. The brand for mashed potatoes," she explained, slanting him a curious look. "The directions call for milk and butter."

"Of course." His stomach churned, and a damnable muscle in his cheek ticked. "I'll have to pay better attention next time."

He could tell his comment puzzled her, but to his relief she let their conversation about mashed potatoes drop. Instead, she turned her attention to Andrew. "So, what are we going to do for your birthday?" she asked him.

"I want a big party," he said, indicating with the stretching of his arms just how big he wanted the get-together to be. "The biggest ever, with you and Dad, my friends from school and Grandpa and Grandma Linden."

Kane put his fork on his empty plate, hating to be the one to crush his son's hopes. "Andy, you know Grandpa and Grandma are planning on giving you a party on your birthday Thursday evening."

His chin shot up a notch. "Will you be there?"

He never was. He'd never been invited to the yearly birthday bash the Lindens held in their grandson's honor, and although he knew they wouldn't make a scene if he went, he preferred to spare Andrew the obvious tension between adults on his special day. A weary sigh escaped him. "No, I won't be there, but we'll spend Friday together. Maybe we can go get a pizza, play some arcade games, then go to the ice-cream parlor for a banana split."

Andy wasn't falling for the subtle bribe. "That's not the same, Dad."

But that's the way it was and had been for the past five years. He didn't have the mental energy to break tradition. Sensing Megan's gaze on him, he glanced at her, expecting to see condemnation in her blue eyes for his nonparticipation. He had every intention of shooting her a mind-your-own-business kind of look, but the honest-to-goodness caring softening her expression stopped him cold.

Abruptly, he pushed back his chair and stood, suddenly feeling suffocated. He didn't want this woman's compassion, didn't like her probing where he was most vulnerable. He barely knew her and didn't like that she could affect him so strongly.

"If you'll excuse me, I have work to do in my workshop." Giving her a curt nod and ignoring her startled expression, he turned and left the kitchen.

CHAPTER TWO

Two days, and his house smelled like *her,* a light, floral fragrance that teased his senses and went straight to his head faster than a shot of one-hundred-proof whiskey.

Two days, and she'd worked her way into his son's heart and brought laughter to his home. Every time he turned around she was there, smiling and talking to him in that sweet voice of hers. And damn, but she made the most delicious beef stew and corn bread he'd ever tasted, all from scratch.

One week? He didn't stand a chance, not when every time she spoke he wondered what her lips tasted like. She reminded him how much he'd liked being married and having a wife to fill the emptiness in the house at night...that first six months when he'd thought life couldn't be more perfect.

He'd disillusioned himself big-time.

With a low growl of frustration, Kane scrubbed a piece of sandpaper over the flat surface of wood he'd cut for a shelf. Other than the handshake he'd shared with Megan the day she'd arrived, he wouldn't be touching her. His personal stakes were too high to risk. Distance would save his sanity and protect his emotions. It had for years.

Shaking his head, he walked to the open barn doors and glanced at the house. The soft glow of lights illuminating the living room window beckoned him. He'd managed to make himself scarce for the remainder of Friday night and all day Saturday to give Andy and Megan time alone to get acquainted. Knowing he couldn't be a recluse forever, he went inside his workshop and put his tools away. He made his way to the house, moonlight guiding the way.

He stepped into the kitchen. An upbeat Alan Jackson tune drifted through the house, along with feminine laugh-

21

ter and boyish giggles. He entered the living room and found them two-stepping to the lively music, an arm's length separating them. Where his son's movements were stiff and awkward, Megan's were fluid and graceful. Whenever Andy stumbled or missed a beat, they'd both burst out laughing, she'd tease him, and they kept going.

Enjoying the scene and his son's eagerness to learn, he leaned against the doorjamb and watched them shuffle around the small room. She wore black leggings that molded her trim bottom and long legs and a white blouse, the ends tied in a knot at her tiny waist. She'd put her shoulder-length hair in a ponytail, and a few shorter strands wisped around her flushed face. Desire and longing mingled, reminding him that he was still a healthy, red-blooded male who appreciated a beautiful woman.

At the end of the song she unexpectedly twirled Andy in a circle. His son's arms didn't coordinate with his legs, and he fell toward Megan, tangling himself in her arms. She lost her footing, and with a surprised cry they landed on the couch. Before Andy could recover from the fall, she began tickling him. Squeals and infectious laughter rang out. Caught up in the fun, Kane chuckled.

She stopped her tickle torture and immediately sat up, her eyes wide and luminous. "I didn't hear you come in," she said breathlessly, smoothing strands of hair from her face.

Her blouse was bunched beneath her breasts, revealing two inches of skin he knew would be baby soft to the touch. Prying his eyes from the temptation, he approached the couch. "You guys were having too good a time."

"Megan was teaching me how to two-step," Andy said, a big grin spreading across his face. "It's fun. Why don't you try it, Dad?"

He tensed. "I don't dance." Working to help support him and his sister had stolen the years when he should have been enjoying school dances and attending town socials. The one and only time he'd danced was at his wedding, and even then it had been a slow, shuffling rhythm he'd feigned, nothing nearly so complicated as all the fancy steps they'd been executing.

"Everybody dances, Dad." He tugged Kane two steps closer to Megan. "Isn't that what you told me, Megan?"

Her startled gaze darted from Kane to their little mediator. She shifted on her bare feet. "Uh, yes, I guess I did."

Kane held up his hands to ward off what he knew was coming. "Son, I have two left feet—"

"And Megan has two *right* feet." Gales of laughter escaped Andy, and he slapped his leg at his silly pun. "Stop worryin', Dad, you'll do fine. It's really easy. All you have to do is put one hand on Megan's waist and hold her other hand, and Megan will put her hand on your shoulder." As Andy spouted the instructions he positioned them accordingly.

Before Kane knew it, he had his hands all over Megan, and although it was all innocent fun, his thoughts were anything but pure. His thumb slipped beneath the loose hem of her blouse and grazed the skin between the waistband of her leggings and her breasts. Yep, softer than skin on a peach. He felt her shiver, saw the awareness in her gaze. He tormented himself further and pulled in a deep breath, filling himself with her scent.

So much for not touching her. So much for keeping his distance, at least physically.

"Now follow Megan's lead," Andy said, just as a new song started on the portable radio sitting on the brick hearth.

A smile trembled on Megan's lips, then a determined I-can-do-this-and-not-be-affected look entered her eyes. With all the primness and professionalism of a dance teacher, she instructed him on the few steps it took to make the two-step possible.

The pattern was simpler than he'd thought. After their first pass around the living room without making too much of a fool of himself, he turned Megan around and smoothly took the lead.

Andy clapped gleefully from the couch. "You're two-stepping, Dad!"

His mouth twitched. "Yeah, I guess I am."

They two-stepped to an upbeat tune without him stumbling or losing count of his steps too often. When the fast country tune segued into a slow, romantic ballad, she started to pull away, her fingers sliding from his shoulder down his arm. He surprised himself by tightening the hand on her waist, keeping her there with the slight pressure. As irrational and telling as the action was, he wasn't ready to let her go. He couldn't remember the last time he'd enjoyed himself so much with a woman.

Her sudden curious expression prompted a bit of daring and recklessness. "Do the same rules apply for a slow song? This much distance, I mean?"

Megan stared at Kane, her heart fluttering like a trapped butterfly in a cage. "They can, but usually…" She looked away. His gaze was too intense, too sexy, and beyond all the dark sensuality she detected a loneliness and pain matching her own, though she didn't know the source of his, nor did he give her any indication he was willing to share it. If anything, he tried much too hard to hide the hurt behind an I-don't-give-a-damn facade. But it was there for anyone who cared enough to look beyond the surface.

And dammit, she cared. Unwisely. Foolishly.

"Usually, what?"

His husky voice brought her back to the present, the distance separating them and what he intended to do about it. She swallowed the knot in her throat and concentrated on the light stubble grazing his jaw, the cute crease in his chin, his lips…no, not his lips. She bravely lifted her gaze to his eyes. "If we were…intimate, the man could pull the woman closer."

He swept a hand down her back in a slow, languid caress and guided her close, his mouth near her ear. "Like this?"

She closed her eyes, suppressing the urge to groan as softness pressed into the unyielding, muscular planes of a body honed by hard, physical work. "Yes."

The light in the living room clicked off, leaving the dim glow from the kitchen as their only source of illumination.

"Adds to the romantic atphost…atmostfear," the guilty party said, sounding perfectly pleased with himself.

"I agree," Kane murmured.

The mellow song played on. Kane smelled like wood shavings, earthy maleness and heat. She absorbed it all. Her hand crept up his arm and gradually settled around his neck, her fingers close enough to sift through the rebel-long strands of his hair. Their bodies moved as one, slow and sultry.

"You lied," she whispered, lost in the magical spell weaving around them.

"I did?"

She leaned back to look at him. He towered a good seven inches over her five-foot-six. She wasn't intimidated by his size. Instead, she felt protected and cherished and very powerful in her femininity. "You've got great…rhythm."

He lifted a brow, amusement and something infinitely more flammable sparking the depths. "Yeah?"

A lazy smile curled her mouth. "You're a natural."

The big hand holding hers squeezed gently. "I'm a quick learner when the subject interests me."

Her heart skipped a beat.

The song ended, and they stopped moving, though their bodies still brushed, an erotic caress that sizzled along her nerve endings. Kane's gaze dropped to her mouth. Self-consciously, she dampened her bottom lip with her tongue. Heated desire flashed in his eyes, and he drew in a ragged breath, as if he was a drowning man trying to hold onto the frayed ends of a rope.

She thought she heard Andrew whisper, "Come on, Dad, kiss her."

There was enough promise and hunger in Kane's eyes that she wanted him to. Her lips parted, and her breathing deepened.

As if coming out of a trance, Kane shook his head and stepped away, severing all contact with her. A rush of chilly air feathered across her arms, leaving goose-bumps in its wake. This time, there was no mistaking Andy's mumbled but clearly disappointed, "Darn it."

Oddly enough, Andy's sentiment echoed Megan's thoughts. A wry smile touched her lips.

Kane turned toward Andy, his face an expressionless mask. "I think you've had enough excitement for today. Time for bed, sport."

"Aw, Dad, can't I stay up a little longer?" Andy asked, shoulders sagging. "I don't have school tomorrow."

Kane turned off the radio and glanced at the clock on the mantel, his movements brusque. "It's nine-thirty. You've been up an hour later than your normal bedtime, and we have church tomorrow morning."

Andy slid off the couch without further argument. "Will you tuck me in, Megan?"

"I'd like that." She brushed a blond lock of hair from his brow, knowing she'd do anything for this little boy. And realizing, too, that his father was making his mark on her, as well, whether he meant to or not. "You go brush your teeth and put on your pajamas. I'll be right there."

Andrew grinned, his eyes sparkling with renewed enthusiasm. "Okay." He scampered down the hall to the bathroom.

Once he was out of earshot, Megan reached out and touched Kane's arm. His entire body tensed, and she immediately dropped her hand. A troubled frown creased his brow, warring with the need in his eyes.

"Kane—"

His hands flexed at his sides. "It was only a dance, Megan." His voice was rough, like the sandpaper he used on his wood.

It had been more than a dance, and they both knew it. After a few long minutes of silence, Megan turned and went down the hallway.

Andrew bounded into bed as she entered his room. He'd changed into a pair of flannel pajamas, his face was freshly scrubbed, and he smelled like mint toothpaste. He slipped beneath the covers, unable to contain a sleepy yawn.

Smiling, she sat on the edge of the mattress beside him. "You have sweet dreams."

"I will." Unexpectedly, he sat up and launched himself at her, hugging her tight around the waist. "I love you, Megan."

Warmth flooded her, reaching places that had been cold and empty for so long. "I love you, too, Andrew."

Kane hesitated at the doorway to his son's room, not wanting to interrupt the tender scene. He propped his shoulder against the frame, giving them a few minutes before he intruded. Andrew thanked her for a fun day, and the smile on Megan's face radiated deep affection.

Andrew settled into bed, and Megan arranged the blanket around him. Just when she would have stood to leave, Andrew grabbed her arm.

"What is it?" she asked.

"Would you..." His voice wavered and his throat bobbed. "Would you be my mom?"

Kane was so shocked by his son's question, he couldn't find his voice to respond before Megan did.

"I'd like nothing more than to be your mom, sweetie," she said, gently cupping his cheek in her palm. "But it's not as easy as that."

"Why not?"

"Because your dad will pick a new mom for you someday."

Guilt coiled through Kane. After Cathy's death he hadn't given much thought to Andrew having a motherly influence in his life. He'd believed the two of them had done just fine on their own for nearly six years...until Megan Sanders had entered the picture.

He couldn't deny the healthy, positive effect she had on his son. Andy glowed like never before. But getting married again wasn't on Kane's agenda. Ever. Not even to a woman with blue eyes so deep he wanted to drown in them every day of his life.

He shook off the insane thought and steeled himself against notions of marriage. Dancing so close to Megan—the heat they'd created must have fried his brain cells.

"What if I pick *you* to be my mom?" Andrew persisted, not willing to accept Megan's answer to his question.

She smoothed her hand over his bedspread, thinking. "How about I be your special friend forever?"

Andrew frowned, seemingly not satisfied with that answer, either. "Can you live here forever?"

Megan laughed and fussed with his pillow. "I don't think your father would like that too much."

"Dad likes you." Andy drew his old, battered teddy bear into the crook of his arm. "Did you see him smiling at you while you were dancing?"

"That was a smile?" she teased, tweaking his nose.

Andy giggled, then grew serious. "He wouldn't let you stay if he didn't like you. And he's not always grouchy. It's just that Grandma and Grandpa Linden—"

"Lights out," Kane said, stepping into the room before Andrew could enlighten Megan on his long-standing rift with his in-laws. Megan didn't need to know the only reason the Lindens had anything to do with him was Andy. They'd made it abundantly clear they intended to be an active part of Andrew's life after Cathy's death, despite blaming Kane for their daughter's demise. Not that he'd ever deny the Linden's their only grandchild.

After tucking Andy into bed and turning out the lights, he walked with Megan into the living room. Now that they were alone, an awkward silence stretched between them. The basic manners his mother taught him nudged his conscience. "Would you like something to drink, or would you like to go to bed?"

His gruff question was met by delicately raised brows. A lovely shade of pink colored her complexion. Her gaze skittered toward the hallway leading to his room, and her fingers fluttered to the collar of her blouse. "Go to bed?" Her voice squeaked.

She thought he meant *his* bed. Although the image of

Megan spilled across his mattress induced a heady, warm rush of desire he was finding increasingly hard to ignore, he suspected she'd want more than just a one-night tumble. Which was more than he was willing to give.

He waved a hand toward the couch. "I could pull the sleeper out if you're ready to retire."

"Oh," she said, a soft breath whooshing out of her. "I'm not really tired."

"Then what'll it be? Coffee, hot cocoa or a shot of whiskey?" He was leaning toward the whiskey. A double dose to knock him out for the night so he didn't toss and turn from the same erotic fantasies that robbed him of sleep last night.

She thought for a moment, then an irresistible twinkle brightened her eyes. "Would hot cocoa be too much trouble?"

He shrugged. "I think I can handle boiling hot water."

"Water?" She grimaced. "That's not the way hot cocoa was meant to be made."

Lifting a brow, he casually crossed his arms over his chest. "Andy never complains." Damn, how did she make him enjoy her and their banter so much? Make him forget all the reasons he never established close personal relationships with women?

The spontaneous, upswept look she gave him started a slow burn in his veins. "Maybe Andy never complains because he doesn't know what it's like to have *real* hot cocoa."

Unable to help himself, he chuckled. The sass and exuberance dancing in her eyes coaxed him into giving as good as she dished out. "Since you've been crowned the cook, how 'bout you show me how to make *real* cocoa?"

She accepted his challenge with too much willingness. "Do you have powdered cocoa?"

He stared at her steadily, trying to ignore the subtle tensing of his insides. "What's the difference?"

Her lilting laughter echoed in the small room. She

thought he was joking. He was dead serious. She realized that much when he didn't join in her amusement.

She struggled to contain her mirth and failed. "I guess the packaged stuff will have to do. With milk. Do you have marshmallows?"

The woman wanted marshmallows, of all things. He rolled his eyes. "I think there's some in the cupboard."

"Will you join me?"

How could he refuse such a request? And did he really want to? He hadn't had cocoa since he was a kid, and it was either a warm drink and good company or a lonely, chilled night out in his workshop.

"Lead the way," he said, before he changed his mind.

He followed her into the kitchen and helped her locate the ingredients she needed. She surprised him by being well acclimated to his kitchen and small pantry, and shooed him out of her way. He settled against the counter by the stove, letting her have free rein.

"I'm mostly a night person," she said, filling a pan with milk then lighting the burner. "I'm used to staying up late, sometimes until one or two in the morning."

"That makes two of us." The confession slipped out of its own accord, giving them a mutual foundation of interest to build on.

She found a spoon in a drawer and began stirring the warming milk. "In fact, I usually do my best writing at night."

"You could use the kitchen table and I could leave you alone—"

"Absolutely not! I'm here to rest and relax and enjoy my time with Andy. And you," she added, not an afterthought but a genuine sentiment that reached inside him and grabbed hard. "No work. I can do that anytime and anywhere. Besides, I just made a deadline before I came out. I wrote an adventure about Andy losing one of his teeth and how the tooth fairy forgot to take his tooth and leave him a quarter."

He gaped at her. "You didn't."

Grinning cheekily, she reached for two mugs in the cupboard next to the sink and placed them on the Formica countertop. "Guilty as charged. I capitalized on a great story. A sure winner with the kids."

Kane cringed and groaned, unable to believe his parental absentmindedness had come back to haunt him in form of a mass-market book. "I hope you mentioned somewhere that the guilt-ridden tooth fairy left him five dollars the following night, instead of the usual one-dollar payment."

Laughing, she dumped powdered mix into each of their mugs and added hot milk. Curls of steam filled the distance between them with the sweet scent of chocolate. "Do you have any cinnamon?"

"Cinnamon?" At her nod, he said, "If I do, it would be in the cupboard above the stove with the spices."

She opened the cupboard. Spotting the container with a picture of cinnamon sticks on the label, she stood on tiptoes to reach it, and came up a few inches short. Stepping behind her, he stretched and effortlessly retrieved the small shaker, unintentionally crowding her into the counter. The front of his fly grazed her bottom, and his thighs fitted precisely with hers. She gasped at the intimate contact and spun around, her fingers gripping the counter behind her.

She looked everywhere but at him. "*The Tooth Fairy's Folly* is one of my favorite stories," she said in a rush, then skimmed her bottom lip with her tongue. "I brought an advance copy for Andy's birthday."

He recognized her rambling for the diversion it was. Unfortunately, his unruly hormones liked the curves of her slim figure enough to ignore the attempted aberration. "I'm sure he'll like that." Grabbing her hand, he placed the cinnamon in her palm, letting his fingers linger longer than decorum called for.

Gulping a deep breath, she turned to the mugs and sprinkled cinnamon on the cocoa. "I hope so. You'll have to read the story and see if I did it justice."

He didn't reply because there wasn't much he could say

that wouldn't turn an enjoyable evening into one of his worst nightmares. "Are all your stories about *my* son?"

"Yes." Smiling, she dropped a cluster of small marshmallows into each mug. The white blobs melted together and turned creamy. "The series didn't start out that way. I created it at a time in my life when I needed something to fill my spare time. Your Andy has been a great source of inspiration for my books."

"I never knew Andy was your inspiration," he said quietly.

She gave him a quizzical look. "You haven't read any of the books I've written? The past year has been based on Andrew's escapades."

He shifted under her probing gaze. "I just thought all those stories were common childhood experiences," he said offhandedly.

"I suppose they are, but I try and write them through Andy's eyes. A child's naïveté is precious. When Andy regales me with his tales, I take the best parts and embellish them. I owe a large part of my success to him." She handed him his mug and tilted it toward his lips. "Taste."

He lifted the rim and took a drink, tasting creamy vanilla, rich chocolate and a hint of cinnamon. "Umm," he said, smacking his lips. "This is the best hot chocolate I've ever tasted."

Her expression turned smug. "Just think how much better it'll be with *real* cocoa." Picking up her mug, she sashayed out of the kitchen.

Shaking his head, he followed her.

In the living room, he set his cup on the mantel, then tossed a few logs onto the grate. Within minutes a bright fire crackled in the hearth, taking away the slight chill in the room.

"Is this Andy's mother?"

Kane straightened and glanced at the framed photograph in Megan's hand, the one Cathy's parents had given Andrew so he wouldn't forget his mother. A blonde woman smiled from behind a sheet of clear glass, her brown eyes full of the sparkle and vibrance Kane had first fallen in love with so many years ago. "Yes. That's Cathy."

"Andrew looks a lot like her." She placed the picture on the mantel. "She's very beautiful."

"Yes, she was."

She sat on the couch and curled her legs under her. Fingers wrapped around the ceramic mug, she took a drink, blue eyes peering at him thoughtfully over the rim.

"Andy must miss her very much," she said after a quiet moment.

He stared at the dregs of cocoa in his cup, the snap and crackle of the fire like gunfire to his ears. "Cathy died when Andy was only two. He doesn't remember much about her."

Sadness and sympathy etched her features. "How did she die?"

He glanced up, his jaw automatically hardening. He had to remind himself that Megan was a stranger in Linden, someone who hadn't heard the horrifying rumor about Kane Fielding. She wasn't pointing an accusatory finger, wasn't looking at him in disdain.

She shifted under his intense gaze. "I didn't mean to pry—"

"She drowned in a nearby lake," he said abruptly.

"I'm sorry."

So was he, more than anyone would ever know. "It was a long time ago." He bent to tend the fire, not wanting to relive that dreary, rainy day when Cathy had died. He relived it every time he saw the Lindens. Every time he passed the lake that had stolen her life.

Megan propped her elbows on the couch's armrest, watching as Kane tended the fire. She wondered if he was still grieving over his wife and if that was part of the reason for the shadows and secrets she occasionally glimpsed.

"Have you ever thought about getting married again?" she asked, her voice hushed, yet something—anticipation of his answer—made her chest tighten. Strange, considering she'd only met him two days ago. But she'd known him for a year and a half, she reminded herself, learning from Andrew that a gentle and compassionate person lurked beneath the sometimes brusque facade.

"No." He carelessly tossed another log on the fire, the muscles across his back rippling with the movement. Sparks filtered up the chimney, and heat radiated outward.

"Haven't found the right woman?"

Balancing on the balls of his feet, he stared into the fire. "I haven't been looking."

She couldn't help but wonder if the right one did come along if he'd consider it. Her own marriage had been less than ideal toward the end, but she still believed one could find happiness with someone else. "What about Andrew?"

He glanced over his shoulder at her, one of his rare smiles threatening to make an appearance. "He's too young to get married."

She made a face at him and earned herself a grin. The man could be charming, even humorous when he wanted to be. She suspected he'd deny it if she told him so. "That's not what I meant. Doesn't Andy deserve to have a mom?" She told herself she was only concerned for Andrew's welfare, but the thought of another woman taking *her* place didn't sit well.

A wickedly dark brow arched. "Are you applying for the position?"

Their gazes clung for several heartbeats. He was being facetious, but she couldn't squelch the instinct in her that was rallying to say yes. She wanted to be a daily part of Andrew's life.

She drew her knees up, then wrapped her arms around them. "I only meant that Andrew should have the influence of a mother and father."

His amusement faded. The firelight played over his features, emphasizing the dark stubble grazing his jaw, and shining off his black hair like a tarnished halo. His eyes glittered like fired emeralds, frightening and hauntingly beautiful at the same time. "I'm not looking to get married again," he snapped, straightening to his full height.

"Andrew and I have done fine on our own, until you—"
As he realized what he was saying, he clenched his jaw.

"Came along?" she finished for him, hurt by his lash of
angry words, although she knew she didn't have a right to
be. She meant nothing to him, despite her feelings for his
son and her need to somehow be accepted by him, too. She
was foolish to think she could mean something to him when
it was apparent he shut out anyone who tried to get too
close.

He jammed his fingers through his hair, sat in the recliner
across from the couch and released a harsh breath that whistled between his teeth. "I'm sorry, that was uncalled for."

The apology was stiff and gruff, as if he'd had to dig
deep for it. "I understand." And she did. She'd obviously
touched on a sensitive issue, one that had unearthed the
shadows of pain lingering in the aftermath of his anger.
The urge to go to him, touch him, comfort him was so
strong it nearly overwhelmed her. She hugged her knees
tighter, unwilling to face possible rejection.

Leaning forward, he braced his elbows on his knees. "I
know you care for my son very much, and it's obvious he
returns the feelings. He's lucky to have you as a...friend."

*And what about you Kane Fielding? Do you consider me
a friend?* Averting her gaze, she watched the dying flames
flicker over the logs in the grate, trying to ignore the more
intense heat of Kane's eyes on her and the way her body
responded with a shivery sensation.

"What about you, Megan?"

His quiet question startled her. "What about me?"

His gaze flickered over her face with interest and curiosity. "Have you ever been married?"

"Yes." *I'm sorry, Megan, our marriage is over. Having
a family isn't as important to me as it is to you. Kids will
only get in the way of my legal career.* Her belly clenched
as her husband's insensitive words whispered through her.
"I'm divorced."

He cocked his head, looking boyishly appealing. "What
fool let you slip away?"

She couldn't contain the bitter laughter that escaped her. Phillip Sanders was no fool. A callous jerk, yes, but at least he'd ended their marriage instead of stringing her along with empty promises he never intended to fulfill.

She studied Kane, seeing no ulterior motives in his question. "I'm surprised you think so."

A noncommittal shrug lifted his shoulders. "I may not be in the market for a wife, Megan, but I'm not blind."

The honest compliment, although issued underhandedly, made her smile. If she wasn't careful, she could fall hard for this man who tried so hard to maintain a tough and gruff, don't-get-too-close-to-me attitude.

She wasn't blind, either.

CHAPTER THREE

CRISP bacon and fluffy scrambled eggs sure did beat the heck out of the bowl of cold cereal he usually ate with Andy in the morning. Stomach satisfied, Kane looked at the woman responsible for the delicious breakfast, ready to address the one concern that had nagged him all morning.

He placed his napkin on his empty plate. "I have to warn you, Megan, people are going to talk today."

Turning from the plate she was rinsing in the sink, Megan grabbed a terry towel and dried her hands. A delicate auburn brow rose in surprise, and she glanced at herself, then at him. "Is it my dress?"

Leaning back in his chair, he surveyed the garment in question. The peach floral material made her look soft, pretty and feminine. Her dress was appropriate for church, with tiny pearl buttons enclosing the blouse to her neck and a flowing skirt that reached well below her knees. She looked as chaste as a schoolgirl, but he knew the garments beneath contradicted her conservative appearance. He'd seen her pull the lingerie from her suitcase this morning before she'd gone into the bathroom to take a shower. He couldn't stop imagining her in nothing but those skimpy panties that had looked as sheer as a sigh and a silky bra with more lace than substance.

A surge of heat pooled in his lap, and he shifted in his seat, grateful for the loose khaki pants he wore. And that Andy had gone to wash his face and comb his hair. "Uh, no, the dress looks fine."

A fascinating combination of guile and sass danced in her eyes as she approached him. "My hair, then?" She touched the fancy braid she'd woven with the cinnamon and fire strands.

He gave her credit for making light of the situation, but

he knew too well how damaging the town's speculation could be. She had a right to know what to expect today, or at least be prepared to handle the stares and whispers as she walked by.

Settling herself in the chair across from him, she continued her lighthearted banter. "Do I have egg on my face? Or maybe bacon between my teeth?"

Dammit, she'd pried a smile out of him again. "No, you look fine."

"Then what could everyone possibly have to talk about?"

He sighed, struggling with the words. "Megan, this is a small town, and the people here have definite opinions and aren't afraid to express them, even elaborate on what they perceive to be the truth. Sometimes those opinions hurt other people in the process. I have a feeling we're going to give the gossips something to talk about."

Leaning an elbow on the table, she rested her chin in her palm, seemingly digesting what he'd told her. "Does that bother you?"

"I'm used to it." But as hard as he'd tried, he'd never grown immune.

She tapped her finger against her cheek contemplatively. "So, is it true what they say about small-town gossip, that it spreads fast and furiously?"

"Like wildfire around these parts." And they always seemed to take a special interest in *his* business.

An unladylike snort of disgust escaped her. "Don't they have anything better to do?"

"Depends on whose business it is and just how titillating the gossip. Your staying here is like throwing a hungry pack of wolves a bone."

"Oh, please," she said, rolling her eyes. "We're adults, for goodness sake."

A grim smile thinned his lips. "I'm sure that's *exactly* how they'll see the arrangement."

"If they're that catty, let them—" Her mouth snapped shut, and she visibly bristled like a lioness in defense of

her little cub. "I don't want Andy to suffer any backlash
of me being here."

"He won't."

"But you just said people will talk."

"Andy won't hear any of it. The town, and gossips, are
careful to curb their tongues around the *Linden* grandson."
Kane's biggest fear after Cathy's death was that Andy
would hear the horrific rumors floating around about him,
and believe them. So far, Andy was blissfully ignorant of
his father's reported reputation.

Catching Megan's frown, he said gently, "I just don't
want any of the gossip to hurt you in any way."

"Thank you for caring," she said softly, making him
realize that he *did* care. "But I can handle the heat if you
can."

He shrugged. "Like I said, I'm used to it."

She leaned toward him and winked playfully. "Then
let's go give them something to talk about."

The gossips were out in full force. Walking down the side
aisle of Linden's only church to a vacant pew, Kane heard,
"Who's that woman with Kane?" He knew most of the
crowd attending the Sunday morning service had come to
their own scandalous conclusions about Megan.

They'd arrived a few minutes late because Andy hadn't
been able to find one of his good leather loafers, but their
tardiness worked to his advantage. Everyone was seated
and waiting for Reverend Paul to make his appearance at
the podium, sparing Kane the phoney politeness the hyp-
ocrites of Linden felt obliged to demonstrate to him on the
Sabbath.

Six rows from the front of the sanctuary, Kane paused
to let Megan and Andy file into the empty pew. Andy
breezed by, waving to his best friend, Corey, who sat two
benches behind them. Megan met Kane's gaze, and the radiant smile she gave him left him feeling like he'd been
punched in the gut. Her perfume stirred his senses as she
passed, adding to the heady feeling lingering from her

smile. The effect she had on him was getting totally out of control.

Damn. Giving himself a mental shake, he followed her into the pew and sat next to her. A family of five filtered into the same row and came up one seat short. Everyone shifted to give them more room, and Kane automatically scooted closer to Megan. Their knees bumped, and she quickly crossed her legs, but that didn't keep his thigh from pressing into hers. The cramped quarters forced him to stretch his arm across the back of the bench to keep their shoulders from butting uncomfortably for the next hour.

"Sorry," she said, slanting him an apologetic look.

He wasn't. Sitting so close to her was pure torture, but he couldn't say he didn't like it. Unfortunately, their position appeared very intimate to their avid audience, one of whom was his mother-in-law. She sat on the opposite side of the church two rows ahead, her short blond hair immaculately coifed. She had a perfect view of the three of them if she craned her neck and moved to the left, which she had no compunction about doing in order to stare at Megan. Her icy blue gaze narrowed in disapproval, and her pink painted lips pursed. Her line of vision shifted to him, and he nodded in acknowledgment. Flustered at being caught, she quickly looked toward the altar just as Reverend Paul stepped to the podium.

The next forty minutes passed slowly, and in every minute that ticked by he caught a covert glance aimed at Megan. Finally, Reverend Paul bid them all, "God be with you." The crowd slowly filtered out of the church and into the bright sunshine. People broke off into small clusters to mingle and chat. Lightly touching Megan's elbow when they reached the bottom of the steps, Kane guided her toward a grassy area where his boss from the lumber mill stood with his wife and two young boys.

"I forgot to mention it sooner," Kane said as they neared his boss, "but Andrew spends Sundays with his grandparents."

"It's nice he has a regular day to visit them."

All part of the deal, and something Kane had learned to accept. "He won't be home until later this evening."

She adjusted the strap of her purse on her shoulder. "If you're worried about entertaining me, I'm very capable of finding something to do to keep myself busy for a few hours."

"Great." So why did her plans interest him more than his Sunday afternoon ritual of spending time in his workshop to keep his mind occupied and off how quiet the house was when Andy wasn't around? He should be glad she wouldn't be bothering him.

"Morning, Jeff." Kane shook the hand of the tall blond man who'd been his only true friend over the years. He gave Jeff's wife, Karen, a light kiss on the cheek. "Hello, Karen. You're looking beautiful, as always."

She laughed and shook her head, her blond hair flowing around her shoulders like a cloud of silk. "Flattery will get you everywhere, Kane. Who's your friend?" She openly eyed Megan, a speculative gleam in her brown eyes.

"This is Megan Sanders. Megan, this is my boss, Jeff Gibas, and his wife, Karen. Their two boys are Tanner and Corey." He motioned to the two tow-headed boys playing with Andrew a few yards away. "Jeff runs the lumber mill in town where I work."

Smiling, Megan shook their hands. "Nice to meet you."

"Likewise." Karen gave Kane a sly look. "Shame on you for not telling us you were seeing someone."

"I'm not," he said, quickly defusing her insinuation. "This is Andy's penpal."

Jeff chuckled, raising a brow incredulously. "Penpal?"

"I write a children's series called Andy's Adventures," Megan explained. "Andrew and I have been corresponding for quite some time now. I'm here for his birthday."

"Oh." Karen didn't look totally convinced, or else she wanted to believe something more significant was going on between him and Megan. "Well, welcome to Linden, Megan. If you get a chance, we'd love to have you and Kane and Andrew over for dinner."

"I don't think she'll have time for that," Kane said before Megan could reply. He shuddered to imagine Karen alone with Megan. He was fond of Karen, but knew from her many comments about his lack of "female companionship" that she wouldn't hesitate to do a little matchmaking.

"See, I told ya she'd come, Corey," Andy said smugly, coming up beside Megan.

"Wow." Blond, hazel-eyed Corey stared at Megan as if star-struck. "Are you really Megan Sanders, the one who writes the books?"

She smiled, totally oblivious of the pedestal her young fans had put her upon. "Yes, I am."

"Awesome." A slow smile crept across Corey's face. "Do you think you could write a book about a boy named Corey?"

She thought for a moment. "I'm pretty busy with my Andy series, but I don't see why I can't give Andy a friend named Corey."

Eyes as wide as half-dollars, Corey turned to Andrew. "Did you hear that, Andy? I'm going to be your friend in her book."

Andy gave Corey a high five. "See, I told you she was cool."

They stood talking for a few more minutes until Andrew grabbed Megan's hand excitedly. "There's Grandma and Grandpa. Come on, Megan, I want you to meet them."

Kane shoved his hands into his trouser pockets and watched them go, struggling with the urge to tell Megan to stay. Patricia Linden never had anything good to say about her son-in-law, and a part of him hated that Megan would be subjected to that censure.

Karen smacked him lightly on the arm with her small purse, bringing him around. "You're just going to stand here and let Andrew feed her to the barracuda?"

"Megan's a big girl, Karen, and more than capable of taking care of herself." It hadn't taken him long to learn that. Megan was a strong individual in character and spirit, and he was confident she could handle anything the barracuda dished out. "Besides, Patricia's problem isn't with Megan, but me."

"Not judging by that viperous glare she's giving Megan."

He refused to take Karen's bait and turn to look. Besides, he'd never been any good at saving damsels in distress.

Megan glanced one last time over her shoulder at Kane before facing the two people who seemed to bring so much joy to one little boy and so much heartache to one grown man. She'd yet to discover what the problem was, but she got the distinct impression the topic wasn't up for discussion.

They stopped in front of the older couple, who looked the epitome of wealth in their Sunday finery. The woman's cool, assessing gaze swept the length of her, scathing in its intensity. The older man observed her with a reserved curiosity, apparently not having condemned her, as his wife instantly had. At least not yet, Megan thought, expecting the worst. The surreptitious glances cast their way by townsfolk, as if they anticipated a showdown of some sort, both amused and annoyed Megan.

"Grandma and Grandpa, this is my bestest friend, Megan Sanders," Andy announced proudly, a dimple appearing in his cheek.

Patricia Linden sniffed indelicately, her gaze darkening with disdain. "You really came."

Megan manufactured a smile for Kane's in-laws, determined to be gracious despite the tension humming between her and the older couple. "I'm pleased to meet you, Mrs. Linden."

Patricia looked at Megan's extended hand as if it were a snake rearing its head. The woman blatantly ignored her attempt at pleasantry, but Megan held her hand steady, unwilling to let Patricia intimidate her. A silent battle of wills ensued.

After long, uncomfortable seconds passed with neither one giving in, a large masculine hand slipped into Megan's, firm and warm in its grip. "I'm Harold, Andy's grandpa. Welcome to Linden."

Patricia glared at her husband. He smiled at her, unaffected by her simmering outrage.

"Megan's staying with us and we're having a blast together," Andy said, a huge grin encompassing his face. "She even taught me and Dad to dance."

"She's staying at the house?" The question wheezed out of Patricia.

Not caring for the way Patricia talked as though she wasn't there, Megan opened her mouth to explain the situation and defend Kane's respectability, if need be.

Andy beat her to the punch. "Dad said she could."

Megan inwardly groaned, imagining by the woman's widening eyes that she was thinking all sorts of sordid things.

"How convenient," Patricia said, her tone snide.

Harold placed a hand on his wife's shoulder. "Patty—"

Patricia shrugged off her husband's touch, her chin lifting haughtily. Her gaze drifted past Megan toward where Kane stood, then back again. Animosity glittered in the depths of her eyes. "How long do you intend to stay in Linden, Ms. Sanders?"

Megan held her growing annoyance in check. "At least a week."

Patricia huffed, bosom rising and falling in indignation. "That's hardly an appropriate arrangement for my grandson—"

Harold stepped forward, dispelling the argument his wife was trying to instigate. "So, sonny boy, you ready to spend the day fishing with your grandpa?"

Andy hesitated and glanced at Megan, his brow furrowed. "Can Megan come with us?"

"Sundays are *our* day together, Andrew," Patricia interrupted, a tight smile pinching her lips. "Don't you want to spend the afternoon with your grandpa?"

Andy looked confused by his grandma's harsh tone. His

bottom lip quivered. "Yeah, but I just thought Megan could come, too."

Megan's heart ripped in two. Bending to his level, she gave him a bright smile and gently nudged him under the chin. "Andrew, I have plenty to do to keep me busy, and I'll be there when you get home." She smoothed his hair and kissed his cheek, hating that he was torn between duty and his real desire. Hating, too, that the Lindens didn't include Kane in their lives. He should be the one joining in on the fishing trip, but he clearly wasn't welcome. Megan ached for Kane. Having grown up in foster homes, she knew the pain of being the outsider always looking in. She knew they had that much in common.

Patricia wiggled her fingers at her grandson. "Come along, it's getting warm, and you know Grandma can't handle much sun."

Reluctantly, Andy placed his hand in his grandma's.

Harold ran his palm over his sparse gray hair, his gaze expressing the apology he wouldn't voice in front of his wife. Megan stood there as the three of them walked away, wondering what awful occurrence had caused such a chasm between the Lindens and Kane.

Andrew glanced over his shoulder at her. "Bye, Megan." His voice was choked with tears.

She fought a swell of emotion. "Bye, sweetheart. Catch me a big fish." She blew him a kiss, and he reached out and grabbed it. A smile chased away the gloom in his eyes, and he tucked the token of affection into his pocket.

Heavyhearted, she turned to where she'd left Kane, surprised to find him alone. Most of the congregation had left, and the ones who'd watched her encounter with the Lindens now headed toward their cars. Apparently, the day's excitement was over.

She rubbed the throb starting in her temple, feeling as though she'd been whirled through a hurricane. Was this the kind of confrontation Kane had to deal with every time he met with his in-laws? And didn't they all realize Andy was the one who suffered from whatever had torn them apart?

As she neared Kane, their gazes met, his watchful and brooding. He'd loosened his tie, and his hair looked like it had been repeatedly finger combed. Back braced against the trunk of the huge shade tree dominating the yard, he looked like a rebel and very unapproachable. He put on a great facade for the rest of the town, but she had no problem stepping beyond the invisible boundaries he'd established. His scowl was worse than his bite.

She stopped in front of him, close enough to touch his hardened jaw. She kept her hands to herself. "Pleasant people, the Lindens are," she said wryly.

"My sentiments exactly," he drawled mockingly, watching as the Lindens's cream colored Cadillac pulled out of the parking lot. Pushing away from the tree, he started toward Megan's car.

She quickly followed, digging her keys from her purse. Catching up to him, she took a risk and asked, "What happened between you and the Lindens?"

He halted at the passenger side of her car. For a flash of a moment she thought he was going to divulge the truth, but instead a bitter smile quirked his mouth. "It's a long story, Megan, and you only have five days left of your vacation." He opened the door, slid into the front seat and enclosed himself in the car.

Realizing that was his way of politely saying mind your own business, she made a face at him through the window. He stared straight ahead, waiting for her to get into the driver's side.

Stubborn man. Long story or not, she planned to take advantage of every one of her five days. The least she could do for Andy before she left was give him the gift of a complete family.

Three honks from the Cadillac signaled the end of Andrew's day with his grandparents and Kane's self-imposed exile in his workshop so he wouldn't have to be alone with Megan. After this morning's debacle at the church, he got the distinct impression she wasn't going to let her question about his relationship with the Lindens die. He had no desire to relive the past. Nor did he care to see Megan look at him with disgust.

Wiping sweat and sawdust from his brow with the back of his hand, Kane rounded the entrance of the barn to meet Andrew, as was his weekly custom, and abruptly stopped.

Megan was already out of the house and halfway down the drive, with Andrew racing toward her. Once Andy was in her arms giving her a fierce hug, the Lindens merged the Cadillac into the street, leaving behind a thin veil of dust, the only sign that they'd been there. Kane had grown used to the unorthodox procedure his mother-in-law had established, but the appalled look on Megan's face as they drove away without a backward glance or an obligatory wave goodbye made him realize just how cold and emotionless their agreement was.

He watched Megan say something to Andy. His son nodded obediently and headed toward the house. Megan started for the barn, her stride purposeful. Instinctively knowing this wasn't a social visit, he resisted the urge to slip inside the barn and switch on his power saw for a few hours to drone out the lecture sure to come.

"Dinner's just about ready," she said, pushing her hands into the back pockets of the faded jeans she'd changed into. The movement stretched the soft cotton of her sweatshirt across her breasts, emphasizing their fullness. "You must be starved, considering you skipped lunch."

"I am," he admitted, unable to miss the sardonic note to her voice that told him she knew he'd avoided her. "I'll be up to the house as soon as I put my tools away." He turned to go into the barn.

"Do they always pull up to the mailbox and honk?"

Her question stopped him before he could escape. He faced her again. "Every week," he said flatly.

Megan watched Kane's defenses rise like a physical cloak of armor and paid them no heed. She was too intent on discovering the facts that still eluded her. "Don't they ever come in, or at least chat for a bit?"

"Nope."

Unable to believe the lengths to which the three of them went to avoid one another, she let the day's accumulation of frustration seep out. "The three of you are being stubborn and selfish."

Dark eyes flashed tempered anger, but his voice was deceptively calm when he spoke. "You know nothing about the situation."

Maybe she didn't, but it wasn't difficult to draw an educated conclusion about their relationship. "I know that Andy is the one suffering while the three of you circle each other like wary cats."

The light filtering from the barn silhouetted his frame, making him appear like a menacing giant in front of her. "Andy is the *only* reason the Lindens have anything to do with me."

Why? She wanted ask, but knew by the heat in his gaze her question would go unanswered. "Other than you, Harold and Patricia are the only family Andy has. Surely the three of you could try a little harder to get along."

"Andy has an aunt," he said defensively.

She remembered Andy mentioning Aunt Diane during one of their phone conversations. She lived in Idaho with her husband. He'd told her that Grandma and Grandpa Fielding had died before he'd been born. She wondered about Kane's relationship with his sister but knew now wasn't the time to pursue her curiosity.

"That's not the same," she argued. "The Lindens are, and always will be, an active, direct part of Andy's life since you live in the same town. Are you going to spend the rest of your lives barely being civil to one another?"

He didn't answer her, just jammed his hands on his hips and glared.

"It's not fair to Andrew," she said on a softer note. "The strain between you and the Lindens is obvious and has got to affect Andrew on some level."

Harsh laughter escaped him. "You must have a nice, *cozy* family."

His taunt cut right to her heart. He couldn't know how lonely and painful her childhood had been, she told herself, tucking her arms over her stomach. "Quite the opposite, Kane," she said quietly. "From the age of eight, when both my parents were killed in a car accident, I grew up in more foster homes than I can remember. I never had a family after that."

Sympathy flickered in his gaze, and he released a tight breath that sounded close to a curse. "I'm sorry."

"Don't be. That's why I see the importance of having one. Surely whatever has come between you and the Lindens can be reconciled."

A muscle in his jaw ticked. "Reconciliation isn't in the Lindens's vocabulary."

How about his? "Couldn't you at least try—"

"No." The one word boomed like thunder in the barn. He leaned close, the sudden dangerous glint in his eyes masking the flash of raw, vulnerable pain she'd seen seconds before. "You know nothing about it, Megan," he said, his voice low with warning. "So leave it alone." He turned and walked away.

If she was smart, she'd follow his advice. Unfortunately, the higher emotional stakes she'd invested in father and son in the year and a half she'd been corresponding with Andy overruled her common sense. As outrageous and foolish as it seemed, she was falling in love with Kane Fielding.

Taking a deep breath of clean, fresh air, Megan plucked another weed from the planter bordering the house, content with a chore most of the women she knew would blanch at. After her divorce, the only friend who'd remained a compassionate listener and adviser was her roommate, Judi Melvin. They'd met years before she'd married Phillip, and their friendship had stayed constant throughout her divorce, when she'd needed a listening ear the most.

Megan was used to being alone, preferred it most of the

time. But the past few days with Andrew made her empty life seem that much lonelier. She didn't relish returning to a small apartment in the hubbub of Seattle, her day-to-day existence broken by a friendly chat with her editor or an occasional visit from a friend. She especially didn't want to revert to weekly letters from Andy and infrequent phone calls, when she'd lived the pure heaven of seeing and talking to him daily.

Sighing heavily, she sank her fingers into the soft soil, sifting out the patches of bright green clover vying for space with the weeds. Tomorrow, after Kane left for work and Andy went to school, she was going to the hardware store to buy some flowers and plant them. Give the house a more cheerful appearance. That would keep her busy until they returned home and she could share Andy's day with him.

She pushed a strand of hair from her cheek with the back of her hand and smiled, remembering her time at school with Andy that morning. He'd been so excited, and his classmates had been polite but not shy about asking her questions about her books. Most of them read her series because of Andrew's prompting. Mrs. Graham, Andrew's teacher, had been pleasant but reserved, watching her in the same speculative way the people at church had.

Overall, she'd had a fun, interesting morning compared to her frustrating evening last night, when Kane had excused himself after dinner and spent his evening in the barn until she'd finally fallen asleep waiting for him. It wasn't taking her long to learn whenever Kane didn't want to deal with something he sequestered himself in his workshop.

And he obviously didn't like that she'd confronted him about his relationship with the Lindens. The man was hurting, way deep down inside, and she'd gone and pried open wounds that had apparently scabbed over but hadn't completely healed. They never would until Kane resolved whatever was tearing him apart inside. She suspected his turmoil had to do with more than just the Lindens' attitude.

The sound of a car turning into the drive pulled Megan

from her thoughts. Glancing over her shoulder and shielding her eyes from the sun, she frowned as a tall, willowy young woman stepped out of an old blue Ford Mustang. The faded jeans she wore were ripped and frayed in strategic places, and a snug T-shirt displayed every voluptuous curve of her firm young body. Thick black hair fell into soft waves to her waist. Megan estimated her to be in her early twenties, young compared to Megan's thirty-one years but plenty old enough to be a girlfriend of Kane's. Her heart gave a little twist. He'd told her he didn't want to get married again, but that didn't mean the man was a monk.

The woman bounded toward Megan, a dazzling smile lighting up her attractive face. "Howdy," she said amiably, her dark, exotic eyes full of mystery.

Dismissing her pang of jealousy, Megan returned the smile. "Hello." Standing, she dusted her hands and brushed off the grass and dirt clinging to her knees, too aware of her grungy appearance. "If you're looking for Kane, he's not home."

"Kane?" The woman's perfectly arched brows shot up an inch. "Are you kidding? He's never around when I show up. I'm sure he prefers it that way."

"Pardon?" Megan was sure she'd misheard the young woman.

"I'm Joyce, Andy's tutor," she explained. "I tutor him every Monday and Thursday afternoon for an hour."

"Oh." Tutor? Andy hadn't said anything to her about a tutor, nor had Kane. Frowning, she glanced at her watch. "Andy should be home any minute. Would you like to come in for a cool drink?"

Joyce hesitated, but there was enough curiosity in her gaze to contradict her reply. "I don't want to be a bother."

"You aren't." She rubbed at the slight twinge in her back from bending over the planter box. "In fact, it's the perfect excuse to quit for the day." *And to find out why Andy needs a tutor when he told me he got straight As on his last report card.*

Megan led the way into the kitchen. She washed her

hands and retrieved a fresh pitcher of lemonade from the refrigerator.

Joyce slid into a chair at the table, a Cheshire cat grin lifting her lips. "So, it *is* true what they're saying."

Megan's senses went on full alert, but her hand remained steady as she poured the pale yellow liquid into two tall glasses. She met Joyce's gaze from across the counter separating them. "Who's saying what?" she asked evenly.

Joyce blinked at Megan innocently. "The townspeople, that you're living with Kane."

Megan groaned. Kane had warned her this would happen. "Just to set the record straight, I'm not *living* here. I'm visiting Andrew."

"Oh," Joyce said quietly, though it was obvious by the gleam in her eyes that she'd formed her own opinion about the living arrangements, which coincided with the rest of the town's.

Tamping her frustration, Megan carried the two glasses of cold lemonade to the table and sat down, eager to change the subject. "Is Andrew having problems in school?"

"No, he's a great student." Joyce's brows creased thoughtfully. "As far as I know he's never gotten anything below an A minus."

"Then why are you here?"

Joyce shrugged and took a drink of lemonade. "Kane insists on having Andy tutored twice a week, and I need the extra cash. If I didn't do it, someone else would."

Megan didn't understand Kane's logic. Why was he so adamant that Andy participate in after-school tutoring he didn't need?

"So what's Kane *really* like?" Joyce asked, her tone husky with interest. "I mean, we all have our own impressions about the man, but no one seems to know the *real* Kane."

The real Kane was kind, sensitive and more vulnerable than he'd admit. He was also breathlessly sexy when she could coax a smile out of him. "He's a good father," she said, hoping *that* bit of gossip made the rounds.

Joyce rolled her eyes, a gust of breathless laughter escaping her. "Surely you see him more than a father figure."

Megan smiled sweetly, deliberately being naive. "I'm not sure I know what you mean."

Seemingly eager to collect and distribute her share of gossip, Joyce fell for the pretense. "You mean to tell me you don't think Kane is drop-dead gorgeous?"

"He's very good-looking." Megan couldn't lie, but a handsome face and a great body weren't all she saw when she looked at Kane.

Joyce hmphed in disgust. "Lord knows I've tried to catch his eye, but he hasn't shown an ounce of interest." Sighing heavily, she reclined in her chair and twirled a strand of hair around her finger. "He just pays me my tutoring fee and doesn't give me a second glance. Most of the single women in town would love to date him, but he's so moody and distant. And, well, then there's the incident with his wife—"

"What incident?" Megan interrupted, more interested in something involving Kane than Joyce regaling her attempts at seduction.

Joyce's eyes widened. "You haven't heard?"

Sensing she was on the edge of something that could possibly be the key to unlocking a part of Kane's personality, anticipation tightened Megan's chest until it hurt. "Heard what?"

A sly smile quirked the other woman's mouth. Pressing a hand to her bosom, she leaned toward Megan and dropped her voice to a whisper. "He killed his wife."

CHAPTER FOUR

HE KILLED his wife.

Megan's heart skipped a beat. The terrifying statement sent chills skittering across the surface of her skin whenever she thought of such a heinous crime.

There has to be a logical explanation, she told herself for the hundredth time. Ever since Joyce had tilted Megan's world on its axis with her outrageous claim, Megan had repeated those soothing words. Andrew had arrived home from school, leaving Megan suspended somewhere between horror and disbelief while Joyce had ushered him into the living room to begin their lessons.

Numbed by shock, Megan had started dinner in a fog like state, her mind mulling over the accusation, then finally rejecting it. If Kane was a murderer, he'd be behind bars, she reasoned. But there were a few questions she hadn't been able to resolve, like why people had fabricated such a horrible, damaging allegation and why Kane allowed such a nasty rumor to circulate.

"The table is all cleared, Megan."

Shaking off the remnants of this afternoon's stunning discovery, she turned from the kitchen sink and lifted the dirty dinner plates from Andy's helping hands. She placed them in the soapy water to soak. "Thank you, honey."

A dimpled grin creased his face. "You're welcome." Grabbing a dish towel from a drawer, he pitched in to help by drying the pans draining on the counter rack.

"Where's your father?" Had he escaped to his sanctuary so early? she wondered.

"He went to take a shower." Andy dried a plate and stacked it on top of a clean one on the counter. "He promised me we'd play a game of checkers before I go to bed."

"That sounds like fun." Smiling at him, she dunked her

hands into the soapy water and scrubbed a pan. More quietly, she asked, "Why didn't you tell me you had a tutor?"

His face reddened and he looked away, mumbling, "Because I didn't want you to think I was stupid."

Understanding his embarrassment, she dried her hands on a spare dish towel and tucked his chin between her thumb and forefinger. She brought his bright brown gaze to hers. "Andy, you could tell me anything at all, even that you were a man from Mars, and I'd *never* think you were stupid."

Her teasing approach prodded a shy smile from him. "Then why do I need *her?* All she does is quiz me on my spelling words for the week and help me with my homework, which I already know how to do. And she makes me read out loud to her. She said Dad told her to make sure we read at least two chapters of a book each session. I can do all that stuff without her."

A valid point, Megan conceded. "Why don't you ask your father why he thinks you need a tutor," she suggested.

"I did. He said having a tutor would give me an advantage over the other kids."

"He's right, you know." She affectionately ruffled his hair.

"But I hate it when Joyce comes over." His eyes filled with the sparkle of an idea. "Do you think *you* could talk to Dad about Joyce not coming over anymore?"

His hopeful expression touched her deeply, made her want to say yes. She'd slay the meanest fire-breathing dragon for him if he asked, but she knew she couldn't, and wouldn't, undermine Kane's authority. "No. It's your father's decision, not mine. I know this is hard for you to understand, but he only wants the best for you."

He hung his head in defeat. "That's what Dad says, too."

Megan suppressed a smile. "Why don't you go set up the checkers game, and when I'm finished cleaning up in here I'll bring you and your dad a slice of the apple pie I made today."

"Okay," he said eagerly, his youthful woes temporarily forgotten as he skipped happily from the room.

As soon as Andy was tucked into bed Kane made his way to the front door, intending to spend the next few hours in his workshop. Or at least until Megan fell asleep.

He'd gotten good at avoiding her. Unfortunately, the solitude and cold of the barn hadn't lessened his attraction toward her. If anything, it intensified his awareness of her when they were in the same room. Like now. He could hear her following him, could smell that soft, feminine fragrance of hers that wreaked havoc with his hormones.

He had to get the hell out of the house before he did something incredibly stupid. Like give in to the temptation of touching her again...or kissing that lush mouth of hers. That particular pleasure would be foolish to indulge in, because he didn't think he'd be able to stop at one taste.

Putting a lid on his frustrating thoughts, he yanked his denim jacket from the coatrack by the door and punched his arms through the sleeves.

"Kane?"

His gut clenched at the sweet, husky sound of his name on her lips, but he didn't turn and look at her, fearing that would be his downfall now that their chaperone wasn't around to help him maintain his distance. "Yeah?"

"Can I talk to you?" He detected a slight tremor in her voice.

Ten different excuses came to mind, all of them cowardly and lame. A part of him had known this was coming, had seen the pensive looks she'd been casting at him all evening. He had no desire to rehash their argument about his in-laws. He straightened the collar of his jacket with an impatient flick of his wrist. "If this is about the Lindens—"

"No, it's not," she said quickly.

He faced her, jamming his hands on his hips. "Then what is it?"

She hesitated at his gruff tone, then her chin lifted. "Could we go out on the porch?"

He lifted a questioning brow.

"There's something I want to ask you." Her velvet blue gaze remained steady on his. "Something *personal*."

Something she obviously didn't want Andy to overhear. "Fine, but you might want to put this on." He grabbed an extra jacket and tossed it at her. "It's cool outside."

She slipped on the sheepskin-lined jacket and zipped it, then cuffed the sleeves to her wrist. He knew her scent would cling to the fleece lining. He knew he'd never be able to wear that jacket—his favorite in the winter—without thinking of her.

He flipped on the porch light and ushered her onto the wide veranda. She sat on the swing he'd made for Cathy as a wedding gift. The chain creaked from her slight weight and years of inactivity. He didn't join her. He didn't plan on sticking around long enough to get cozy.

"Is there a problem?" he asked.

"I heard a rumor today." Her voice was a soft, hushed whisper.

His body tensed, and he had to force himself to relax. Bracing his back against the porch post by the stairs, he strove for a flippant attitude. "Let's see, which one might that be? That I'm a horrible father and neglect my son? Or maybe the one about me being a recluse? Then there's the one about how I'm on the verge of bankruptcy—"

"What about the one about you killing your wife?" she asked calmly, though her fingers curled tightly around the swing's intricately carved wooden armrest.

His heart slammed against his chest, then resumed at a frantic pace. Sweet Lord, he could have dealt with any one of them but that one. He could have coped with *anything* but the tenderness and understanding in her gaze. She was waiting, *hoping* he'd deny the accusation.

"It isn't a rumor." He forced the words out, his voice rough and raspy.

Fear flashed across her features, then just as quickly anger took its place. "I'd appreciate it if you didn't ridicule me."

She thought he was joking. Bitter laughter spilled out of him. "You don't know the first thing about me, Megan, except for what Andy has told you. And what you don't know you won't like. So, like the situation with the Lindens, I suggest you leave it alone."

"No." She came out of her seat and toward him, fiery determination etching her features. "I want to know why people would say such a horrible thing."

He glared at her, giving in to the masochistic urge to scare her. "Because maybe there's a bit of truth to it."

"I don't believe it," she said softly and with so much certainty *he* almost believed her.

He compressed his mouth into a thin line and clenched his hands to keep from reaching out to touch her. "Then you're a fool."

A faint, challenging smile lifted her mouth. "*They're* the fools if they believe you're capable of hurting anyone."

But he *had* hurt Cathy, if not physically, then emotionally. The fear that he could do it again to another woman kept him from caving in to Megan's gentleness. "Believe it, Megan," he said harshly, and turned to go.

She grabbed a fistful of his jacket sleeve and pulled him back around with more strength than he would have thought her capable of. "Damn you, quit hiding! You might be able to fool the entire town, but you don't fool me. Whatever happened to Cathy, you weren't responsible. She *drowned*, Kane. You told me so yourself."

"I drove her to it," he said furiously.

"Did you hold her under the water?" she countered heatedly.

Her sarcastic question hit too close to the truth. The fight went out of him, draining away his burning anger. "I might as well have."

She frowned, her eyes brimming with confusion. Letting go of his arm, she stepped back, her gaze searching his face for answers. "I...I don't understand."

Dragging a hand roughly through his hair, Kane turned away. Megan didn't deserve his anger, no matter how long the emotions had been pent up without a release. Finally, someone cared enough to listen to him instead of theorizing about what happened between him and Cathy. The truth squeezed like a vise around his lungs, the pressure nearly unbearable. God, he wanted to tell his side of the story so badly, purge all the bitterness, resentment and guilt eating him up inside.

Blowing out a long, steady breath, he gathered strength. "I met Cathy when I was twenty-three, and she was twenty," he began, moving across the porch away from Megan. If he was going to do this, he had to detach himself from her as much as possible. "Cathy actually pursued me, and despite knowing that her parents expected a better catch than me for their only child, I fell hard for her. She was young, pretty, and fun to be with." And he'd had so little excitement, growing up so quickly. Cathy's vivacity had brightened his dull life and made him feel a little reckless. "Six months after we started dating she got pregnant."

The swing creaked as Megan settled herself onto the bench seat. "I take it the Lindens weren't too happy about that."

He glanced at her, his mouth twisting into a parody of a smile. "Hardly." Being pregnant had come as a shock to Cathy, too, who'd feared her parents' reaction. She'd been so upset, she'd suggested having an abortion. Kane's stomach pitched at the memory. He'd been furious that she would even consider such a heartless alternative. "I wasn't about to give up my child or neglect my responsibility to Cathy. I did love her, and I wanted to marry her."

And for the first six months of their marriage he believed they could be happy together. But after the novelty of being a housewife wore off, Cathy had grown bored and decided she wanted more than Kane's little house, an old truck and living on a budget. She wanted all the luxuries her parents had showered on her, but Kane couldn't afford them on his wages from the sawmill.

Thrusting the tips of his fingers into the front pockets of his jeans, he stared at the moon. "After Andrew was born,

Cathy's father, who's the president of the Linden Trust and Loan bank in town, offered me the position of vice president of operations, with a hefty salary that was more than triple my yearly wages at the sawmill. Cathy *asked* him to give me the job." He couldn't help his sharp tone.

"Regardless, that's quite an offer."

"I couldn't…" His jaw clenched and he bit back his words. "I didn't want the job."

Her voice softened with empathy. "Pride got in the way?"

"Yeah, that was part of it."

"And the other part?"

The other part was too humiliating to reveal. "I hate wearing a suit and tie," he said in answer to her prompting.

She smiled at his smart remark. "That would definitely be a problem, but not something you couldn't adjust to."

This woman sensed too much and was relentless in her pursuit. "Not only did I not want to depend on the Lindens for the rest of my life, or be indebted to them, my experience is limited to scaling trees, cutting footboards and working in the bush. I know nothing about banking or holding an executive position."

"You could have learned," she said, pushing the swing into motion with the toe of her sneaker.

That's what he and Cathy had argued about until he'd finally made her understand that he'd *never* be able to take the fancy banker job or be a successful businessman like her father. "I was more than capable of supporting my family working at the sawmill," he said, repeating the adamant words he'd told Cathy that fateful day.

"But not in the way she was accustomed," she guessed.

"No, but we weren't living in poverty, either," he argued. "I could take care of my own family without the Lindens' help."

"And Cathy resented that."

She'd resented that he'd never be anything more than a blue-collar worker. And she'd been so humiliated she never told her father the real reason Kane had refused the executive position, just let Harold believe his son-in-law snubbed a golden opportunity.

"Her parents resented me and my decision, too. They felt they were just trying to help me better myself. Not taking that damned job was the crux of our marriage. Nothing was the same after that. She hated living here and being married to me and made no secret of her feelings. Her parents blame me for not taking the job, for her depression and ultimately, for her death."

"That's ridiculous!"

Kane didn't think so, considering he could have alleviated her misery but had chosen not to. "She asked for a divorce just after Andrew's second birthday, but I refused to give her one. I didn't want to lose Andrew." Wearily, he dragged a hand over his jaw. "Later that same week she was found in the lake that adjoins my property. She'd drowned."

A gasp echoed from Megan's side of the porch. "Did she…kill herself?"

"Nobody knows." Resting his hip against the porch railing, he rubbed his forehead. A measure of guilt compounded the throbbing in his head. "I don't know what the hell she was doing down by the lake. She didn't know how to swim. She could have slipped and fallen in, she could have jumped in, or somebody could have pushed her in…someone like me."

The rhythmic creaking of the swing came to an abrupt halt. "Stop it," she said, her tone low and vehement.

But he couldn't stop. She'd wanted the sordid details, and he was going to give them to her. Maybe then she'd keep her distance. "I might not have pushed her in physically, but I drove her to it emotionally."

"And it could have been an accidental drowning," she refuted emphatically.

"Yes, but it's easier for everyone who knew Cathy and knew how miserable she was being married to me to believe I killed her."

A frown marred Megan's brow. "That's ludicrous."

"Maybe not. She *was* unhappy, and I have no idea what she was doing out by the lake on a rainy day." And he'd never know, could only live with the guilt, the curious stares and the whispers behind his back.

She left the swing and approached him. He tensed and resisted the impulse to move away before she left him no means of escape. The porch light gave her an ethereal appearance and added to the shimmer of compassion in her gaze. Damn her. His dark soul yearned for the tenderness and understanding he'd never received from his wife, but which Megan offered so openly.

"Don't you understand, Megan?" he asked angrily, wanting to intimidate her so she'd forget about redeeming him. "I could very well have killed Cathy."

She stopped in front of him. Slowly, she reached up and cupped his cheek in her palm. "Quit blaming yourself for something you had no control over."

Her touch was soft and gentle, a balm to his battered and bruised heart. Swallowing the thick need gathering in his throat, he grabbed her wrist and pulled her hand away. The rough movement brought their bodies inches apart. Their gazes locked, hers dark and luminous, not with apprehension but with a wanting that nearly crumbled the walls he'd erected around his heart.

Dammit, he didn't want to care for her, like her, even. Too late for that. She'd gone where no woman had treaded in so long he'd thought he'd lost the capacity to care. Megan Sanders was proving him wrong, forcing him to realize he was a flesh-and-blood man who needed a bit of tenderness.

"Kane," she whispered, her breath so close it became his own.

"No," he said roughly, tightening his hold on her wrist as if the action could keep his emotions leashed just as securely.

What the hell was she doing to him? She looked like an angel, his salvation, and at the moment he'd sell his soul to the devil to bury himself in her exuberance and warmth and claim her for his own.

"*No*," he said again, this time with the strength and conviction that protected his pride. "I'll only hurt you, Megan."

"You don't have it in you."

God, did the woman have no sense? He was trying to warn her, save her from heartache and pain. "I could *destroy* you." Just as he'd destroyed Cathy.

Her gaze remained unfaltering. "Never."

Nope, not a lick of sense. "I don't have the greatest reputation in this town."

A sultry smile curled her mouth. She slipped her hand inside his jacket and pressed her palm against his chest. His heart beat wildly and increased in tempo with the slow slide of her fingers. "Your reputation is overrated," she murmured.

He caught a groan before it escaped. God, did she realize what she was doing to him? That she was turning him inside out and pushing him to the brink of control? "Dammit, Megan, don't waste your time caring about me."

She recklessly ignored his warning. "If you're trying to scare me away, don't bother." She stood on the toes of her sneakers so they were eye to eye, their mouths a whisper apart. "It's too late. I already care." Before he could respond, she softly skimmed her lips across his.

It was the sweetest kiss he'd ever received, honest and pure and filled with everything missing from his life. She didn't care what everyone said about him, wasn't running from him like a smart woman would. Instead, she slid her hands around his neck, sank her fingers into the thick waves breaking over the collar of his jacket and pressed her body to his.

An instant rush of heat swept through his veins. He gripped her hips with his hands to pull her away, but she wasn't going anywhere. "Megan—"

"Stop fighting what we both want so badly," she whispered. She stared deep into his eyes, and he watched blue flames of desire leap to life in her gaze. "Please."

I believe in you. Her unspoken words filled him with a long-forgotten hope and sent him over the precarious edge he'd been teetering on. With a raw groan of surrender, he lowered his mouth to hers and parted her lips with the pressure of his.

Sighing softly, she responded like a thirsty flower, opening to receive the slow, silken glide of his tongue across hers. He drank deeply of her, tasting a seductive blend of cinnamon, apples and a heated passion that made his head spin.

The kiss was hungry, sexy and so thorough it left them both breathless and trembling when Kane finally dragged his mouth from hers. One look at her soft, aroused expression made him consider the pleasure he'd find if he invited her to his bed and took this encounter to its logical, fulfilling conclusion.

Summoning every ounce of restraint, he set her away from him and started toward the stairs. He had to get away before he gave in to the temptation and promise shining in her gaze.

"Kane?"

The uncertainty in her voice tore at him. Schooling his features into a mask of cool indifference, he stopped and looked at her. And wished he hadn't. The confidence she'd displayed moments ago had been replaced by a vulnerability that struck a chord in him. The susceptible emotion spoke volumes, telling him without words she wanted to be needed and loved. By him. The need he could deal with. It was the love part he had a problem with. Other than Andrew, he wasn't willing to risk that part of himself.

But neither did he want to hurt Megan.

That last thought prompted him to temper his words. "I'd be lying if I said I didn't want you, but I'm going to walk away before we do something we regret. You obviously don't know what's bad for you."

She lifted her chin challengingly. "I know what's *good* for me."

A grim smile claimed his lips. "You *think* you do, but, sweetheart, it sure as hell isn't me."

Bleary-eyed, Kane stared at his reflection in the bathroom mirror. He looked like death warmed over, and it was *her* fault. Dark stubble lined his slack jaw, and two bloodshot eyes mocked him.

A sound of disgust rumbled in his chest. He'd spent a sleepless night tossing and turning, wanting Megan with an intensity he couldn't ever remember experiencing before. The wanting went beyond sex and lust to something far more basic and elemental he didn't want to acknowledge or analyze. Something buried and vulnerable and too damned fragile to risk. Even a cold morning shower hadn't eased his hard and aching body. He didn't think the deep craving for her would abate until she left Linden.

He wondered if he'd survive that long.

With a low, frustrated curse, he yanked on his jeans, then his blue chambray work shirt. Determined to keep his testosterone level to a minimum, he shoved his fingers through his damp hair and exited the bathroom. The delicious aroma of fresh brewed coffee greeted him, and he followed the scent, stopping on the way to make sure Andy was up and getting dressed for school.

He walked into the kitchen and headed straight for the coffeepot. Megan stood at the counter, busy writing something on one of Andy's doodle pads. She didn't acknowledge his presence. A moment later, notepad and pencil in hand, she passed him on her way to the refrigerator.

He retrieved a coffee mug, annoyed by her disregard and irritated with himself for allowing her disregard to bother him. He should consider himself lucky she hadn't pitched a mug at his head for his barbaric behavior last night.

"You're up early," he said, sounding more grizzly than he'd intended.

She gave him a smile that didn't quite reach her dark-rimmed eyes. "I couldn't sleep." She inventoried the contents of his refrigerator, then jotted down a few notes.

At least he wasn't alone in his misery, he thought peevishly as he filled his mug with strong, black coffee. Bracing his hip against the counter, he took a drink and watched Megan dominate his kitchen.

She crossed to the cupboards and scanned the staples on the shelves. A knee-length cotton sleep shirt covered her decently— until she stretched to move a few items around. The hem rose to her thighs, revealing slender legs that projected images of him skimming his hand up that smooth, soft skin. She abruptly turned and he lifted his gaze, making it only as far as her perfectly rounded breasts and the pebbled tips that strained against her shirt. His body responded with a rush of desire that tightened the front of his jeans.

So much for keeping his testosterone under control.

He set his mug on the counter with a dull thud, grabbed a box of cereal from the cupboard and brought down a bowl. Breakfast would give him something to focus on.

"You'll have to pass on cereal this morning," she said from behind him. "You're out of milk. I'll get some more today."

He turned and faced her, keeping his eyes above her neck. As if that made any real difference! If only her lips didn't remind him how good she tasted, and how that soft mouth responded with such uninhibited passion. "No," he said through gritted teeth. "*I'll* pick some up after work." The last thing he wanted was to owe her, even for something as simple as groceries.

She glanced up from her list, frowning. "I don't mind—"

"Neither do I." He was being rude and unreasonable but couldn't help himself.

Her mouth pursed and her eyes flashed with a spark of blue fire. "Fine." Ripping off the top sheet of paper from her pad, she thrust it at him. "Then I'll assume you won't mind picking up a few other things for me."

Everything within Kane froze. He stared at the paper she

held out to him, that slow, sickening feeling he despised gradually traveling through his system.

"Take it," she said, forcibly slapping the paper into his hand. "God forbid I should do something nice for you."

"What's this for?" His voice sounded rough even to his own ears.

She gave him an odd look. "Just a few items you're low on and a couple of things I need."

"A couple is *two*." The turbulent emotions twisting through him raised his voice a few decibels. "There are at least fifteen items on this list."

She crossed her arms over her chest. "Is that a problem?"

It sure as hell was. "Is all this really necessary?" he snapped.

She stared at him for a long moment, those incredible blue eyes of hers seeking a reason for his outburst. "Yes, it's all necessary. I promised Andy we'd make chocolate chip cookies," she said, as if that explained the entire list.

How in the hell was he going to get out of this mess? His heart hammered in his chest, and he wanted to roar in frustration. "Won't boxed cookies do?"

"No." She grabbed the list from him, anger tightening her normally soft features. "Since picking up the extra items is such a problem for you, *I'll* handle it." She whirled and marched out of the kitchen, muttering beneath her breath, "Grouch."

He cringed as she shut the bathroom door more forcefully than necessary. A mixture of relief and guilt flooded through him, but before he had a chance to cope with those mixed emotions, Andrew walked into the kitchen, frowning as he glanced from the direction Megan just headed to his dad. Was that a subtle accusation in his gaze, Kane wondered, or was his own remorse making him imagine his son's speculation?

"We're out of milk for cereal," Kane interjected quickly, unwilling to explain his conversation with Megan. "How about a waffle for breakfast?"

"Okay." Sliding into his seat, Andrew dug through the backpack on the chair next to where he sat and withdrew a red piece of paper. He put it on the table where Kane normally sat. "This is for you. I forgot to give it to you last night."

Kane dropped a frozen waffle into the toaster, eyeing the paper from a distance. "What is it?"

"It's an invitation to open house at school next month," he said without much enthusiasm, his gaze fixed on something on the table. "Mrs. Graham needs to know if you'll be going."

"Of course I'll be going." How could Andrew think otherwise? "I haven't missed an open house yet, have I?"

"No," came Andrew's quiet reply.

Kane frowned, wondering what had brought on his son's pensive mood. "You don't seem too excited about open house."

Andy shrugged and finally looked at his father. "I just hope Megan can come."

Ah, now he understood. Remembering the negative signals he'd sent Megan a few nights ago when Andrew had invited her to his open house, he experienced a moment of regret. He'd hurt Megan, but it had been necessary. A one-week vacation was one thing, but Kane didn't think he could survive her insinuating herself in their lives on a permanent basis. Especially after this morning's fiasco.

The browned waffle popped up, and Kane slathered it with butter, added syrup, then set it in front of Andrew. "She said she'd check her schedule when she got home. She might have other plans."

Andy's eyes narrowed perceptively. "You don't want her to come, do you?"

Kane cringed as he poured hot coffee into his mug. "Andy, Megan has her own life in Seattle." *And we have our own lives in Linden, without Megan. I'd like to keep it that way, as much as possible, in order to save my sanity.* "I don't want you to be disappointed if she can't be here."

Defiance lit up Andrew's eyes. "She's my special friend, Dad."

"I know you're fond of Megan—"

"I love her."

Andrew's tone and expression were so serious that Kane found a bit of amusement in his son's devotion until Andy followed it up. "Do *you* love Megan, Dad?"

Kane took a careful drink of coffee. The question was asked innocently, and Kane didn't think his son knew the depth of meaning to the word, but a well of emotions sprung to the surface and demanded his immediate attention. There was caring and need, and even a heady rush of desire…but nothing resembling the heartbreaking emotion of love. *Thank God.* "No, son, I don't."

"Why not? She's nice, and pretty, and she's a good cook."

As if he hadn't noticed. "Andy, Megan *is* nice, and pretty, but it's just not the same thing as love."

Andrew's shoulders slumped. "You just don't know Megan like I do."

Kane knew enough about Megan to realize he *could* fall in love with her if he allowed himself. But he feared letting someone get that close again. Being in love meant trusting someone enough to bare your soul and share secrets. In his experience, the risk wasn't worth the gain.

Feeling a familiar bitterness rise to the surface, Kane dumped the rest of his coffee into the sink and grabbed his truck keys from the counter. He paused momentarily at the kitchen door, knowing he couldn't leave without saying something to Andrew. But he couldn't tell Andrew what he wanted to hear, either.

"Have a good day at school," he said, his tone soft. The woeful way Andrew looked at him nearly made his heart break. "And tell Mrs. Graham I'll be there."

He slipped through the living room and out the front door just as Megan exited the bathroom.

CHAPTER FIVE

"ARE you and Dad mad at each other?"

Megan glanced at Andrew, who stood on a stool next to the counter, spatula in hand. With a weary sigh, she removed a sheet of chocolate chip cookies from the oven. She set them on the stove, thinking back to the night on the porch when the dissension started. "Your father and I had a...little difference of opinion." She pulled off her insulated mitt, put it in the drawer and turned off the oven.

Andy scooped up a warm cookie with his spatula and put it on the cooling rack. "About what?"

About how much a kiss meant. About how two people are skirting around the sensitive issue of how they really feel about one another. "Just grown-up stuff. Nothing for you to worry about."

"But Dad hardly ever talks to you anymore."

"I think he just has a lot on his mind." *Like inventing different ways of avoiding me.*

She'd been shameless in her approach on the porch, but she didn't care, and she didn't regret her actions, not if that's what it took to get through to the stubborn man and make him realize he was good and kind...and certainly not the monster the people of Linden believed him to be. He could no more have killed his wife than he would harm Andrew. She knew it and believed it, so why couldn't he?

Her plan had backfired. While she'd reveled in his earthy, sensual kiss, he'd retreated. He'd warned her to stay away, that she didn't know what was bad for her, but as she'd told him, it was too late. What she felt for Kane was overwhelming and a little frightening in its intensity, but she wouldn't and couldn't deny her growing emotions, despite his continual attempts to push her away. This morning's ridiculous argument was a perfect example of his stubbornness.

Andy stacked warm, fragrant cookies on a small plate. "Maybe you could take Dad some cookies and talk to him," he suggested, licking smeared chocolate from his fingers.

Megan shook her head. "I'd better not."

"Please?" He looked at her with hopeful brown eyes. "Dad *loves* homemade chocolate chip cookies. Maybe if you take him some of yours he won't be so grouchy."

Megan smiled, appreciating Andrew's creative attempt to get her and his father to reconcile. "I doubt cookies will change his attitude," she said, wiping the counter.

He grabbed her arm and waited for her to look at him. "Please, Megan? I want Dad to like you as much as I do."

Gently, she cupped his cheek in her palm, wanting to tell him that you couldn't force someone to like you. The feelings were either there or they weren't. Judging by that kiss, there was a definite spark between her and Kane, but *sex* and *like* were two different issues.

But when Andrew looked at her as if she had hung the moon and stars, she found it difficult to refuse his request. God, she was going to miss him. She knew a huge, empty void would fill her when she left.

Knowing she didn't want to spend the next few days with this awful tension between her and Kane, she smiled at Andrew. "Okay, sweetie, I'll give it a shot."

Andrew threw his arms around Megan's waist and hugged her tight. "Thanks, Megan!"

"Yeah, well, let's just hope your father doesn't bite the hand that feeds him." They broke apart, and Megan tapped his nose. "While I'm talking to your dad, why don't you water those pansies and gardenias I planted out front?"

He gave her a dimpled grin that made her melt. "Okay."

Megan picked up the plate of cookies and headed for the back door, wondering if sweets truly could tame this savage beast.

* * *

The high-pitched whine of a power saw filtering from the barn made Megan wince. She hesitated at the entrance, debating on whether she really wanted to do this when Kane had made it abundantly clear, in his words and actions, that he preferred being alone while she was here.

Shifting on her feet, she glanced over her shoulder. Andy stood at the flower bed, spraying a stream of water at the colorful flowers she'd planted and watching her at the same time. He gave her an encouraging thumbs-up sign, and she knew she couldn't back out now.

Running her fingers through her hair, she drew a deep breath to calm the nerves tumbling in her stomach. She moved into the cool interior of the barn, cookies in hand. Kane's back was to her, and he hadn't heard her enter. She stood there for a moment, discovering a fascination in watching him in an element where he seemed so comfortable.

He grabbed a measuring tape from his worktable and measured the huge slab of pine he'd just cut, then made marks on the wood with a pencil. He put on his protective glasses, hefted the scroll saw and cut out the scalloped edges. The scent of sawdust filled the air, blending with other tangy, woodsy smells. Particles of dust and wood settled on his black hair and broad shoulders.

The muscles beneath Kane's blue chambray shirt bunched and rippled as he maneuvered the saw to his whim. Her gaze drifted lower, to the way soft denim outlined his firm buttocks and strong thighs. The man had an incredible body, powerful and lean and down-to-earth sexy. Her pulse acknowledged the attraction with a sudden flutter.

When he turned the power tool off and set it on the worktable, Megan decided to make her presence known. "What are you making?"

The fingers running over the rough edges of wood stilled but he didn't glance in her direction. "A headboard." His tone was abrupt and flat and didn't encourage conversation.

Megan experienced a twinge of annoyance. Determined to chisel a few notches out of that damned emotional barrier he erected whenever she was near, she walked toward him. "For yourself?"

"For my sister. Her birthday is in July." He pulled off his plastic glasses and tossed them onto the table.

"Diane, right?"

"Yep." Still he didn't look at her.

"Are the two of you close?"

"Close enough," he said brusquely, and grabbed a square piece of sandpaper.

Boy, was he ever a wealth of information, she thought in mild irritation. Prying personal stuff from him was worse than trying to coax a turtle from his shell. "Does she see Andy very often?" she persisted.

He brushed his fingers over the wood he'd just cut, then followed it with the sandpaper, his gaze narrowed on the task. He was quiet for so long, she thought he either hadn't heard her or wasn't going to say anything. Finally, as if he sensed she wouldn't let the question go unanswered, he said, "She hasn't seen him since after Cathy died, but she calls."

Megan was pleased that Andrew at least had a good relationship with his aunt, even if it was a long-distance one.

He continued with his work, ignoring her. She sighed in frustration but wasn't totally discouraged. She glanced at the thick piece of wood Kane intended to shape into a headboard. The pine was smooth except for the raw scalloped edges he'd just cut and was now trying to sand. The potential for an exquisite piece of work was evident in the intricate detail of the design.

Remembering the toys he'd made for Andrew and that Andrew had told her he'd made most of the furniture in the house, she said, "You make beautiful pieces of furniture. Have you ever thought about contracting your work?"

His body visibly tensed. "Nope."

"Well, you should consider it." When he didn't respond, she set the plate of cookies on the table beside him. "I brought a peace offering," she said softly.

He stopped his sanding and finally looked at her, a mocking smile lifting his mouth. "I suppose Andrew sent you out."

"Yes," she admitted, stunned by the heat in his green eyes. The man did an excellent job of keeping his distance emotionally but made no attempt to distance himself from the physical awareness that crackled between them. "But I wanted to talk to you anyway."

Lifting a dark brow, he picked up a cookie and bit into it, chewing slowly. "'Talking' is what got us into trouble the other night. Or have you already forgotten what kind of trouble our conversations lead to?"

She flushed at his bold reference to their kiss and at the way his gaze focused on her lips, but she wasn't about to shy away from his callous manner. "Is that what you call what happened between us? Trouble?"

"I call it a mistake."

Liar, she thought. There had been too much raw need in the way his mouth had taken hers, too much hurt that needed sustenance. She'd given him that much, if only for a brief time.

As if he'd read her mind, his gaze darkened and he said, "If you were smart, you'd forget about that kiss."

That's kind of difficult to do when you branded me straight to my soul. Shaking that thought from her mind, she focused on the reason she'd come out here. "Do you plan to avoid me until I'm gone?"

"I'm gonna try." He tossed another cookie into his mouth.

She didn't know whether to feel indignant or amused by his valiant attempts to keep them separated. "What if I won't let you?"

Bracing a hand on the worktable, he leaned close. "What makes you think you have a choice in the matter?"

"What makes you think *you* do?"

They stood nose to nose, boots to the tips of her espadrilles. Heat and the musky scent of man surrounded her, stirring something within her to vibrant life. Green eyes flashed with a multitude of emotions ranging from anger to passion. Knowing how easily their tempers could flare into desire, her heart picked up its beat.

She blew out a deep breath to release the chaos in her. "Dammit, Kane, do you think we can try and be civil to one another?"

"Why?" His tone brooked no compromise. Neither did his defensive stance.

"For Andrew's sake! He's upset because we aren't talking. I don't want to spend the rest of my vacation walking on eggshells when you're around, or trying to make polite conversation." She rubbed her forehead, forcing herself to calm down. When she looked at Kane again and saw those shadows in his gaze that tugged at her empty soul, she knew she was ready to take a chance at what she felt for him. "I know you don't want to hear this, but I care for you—"

"You know nothing about me, Megan," he said, cutting her off. He turned away and tossed his tools into a metal box.

She wasn't about to let him retreat, not when she'd just bared a part of her heart. Stepping closer, she curled her fingers around his forearm, exposed by the sleeves he'd rolled up. He froze and looked at her with an icy glare.

She wasn't daunted. "I know enough to realize you're a very special man."

His mouth curled into a bitter smile, and he pulled his arm from her grasp. "Yeah, so special I got a line of women knocking down my door."

"Maybe you would if you dropped those damned shields and let someone past this tough facade of yours. You put on a real good act, Kane, but I'm not falling for it."

He dropped a hammer into the metal box with a loud clank and gave her a quick, sweeping glance. "Don't disillusion yourself, sweetheart. What you see is what you get."

"What I see is someone who's been hurt and betrayed. I know that feeling, Kane."

Rough laughter escaped him. "Do you?"

His words would have mocked her if it hadn't been for the pure torment in his eyes. "Yes, I do," she whispered.

He straightened, and she watched him erect those internal barriers that kept him safe from anything that threatened his emotions. She wanted to tear them down, even if it meant risking rejection. What had started as a promise to Andrew had turned into a personal quest.

Now, she was willing to risk her heart. "Have you ever known that something was so right? That what you felt for someone transcended anything you've ever experienced before?"

His jaw clenched. "No."

She bravely upped the stakes despite his denial. "Well, that's how I feel about you."

Part of that fortress crumbled, giving her a glimpse of the vulnerable man beneath. "What do you want from me, Megan?"

What she wanted scared her to death, because she couldn't remember ever feeling so in love with a person. The fear was real, because he wouldn't be an easy man to love, wouldn't let her close enough to love her back. "I...I don't know."

Something dark and indiscernible flared in his gaze. He started toward her, and she instinctively stepped back until her spine pressed against the cool, plank wall of the barn. She had no idea what he intended.

He braced a forearm on the wall by her head, trapping her within the close proximity of his body. "I know what I want from you." His voice was low and raspy.

Her heart raced at the sudden gleam in his eyes. The heat and scent of him filled her nostrils, and she pressed her palms to the wall behind her for support. "What?"

He spread his callused fingers around the base of her neck and pressed his thumb to the erratic pulse in her throat. "To finish what we started the other night."

Damn him, he was trying to frighten her, but she wasn't about to be bullied by his harsh tactics. She lifted her chin and steadily held his gaze. "Then do it," she said.

Surprise, then something wild and reckless were reflected in his expression. Slowly, he framed her face in his large hands and moved closer so his thighs bracketed hers.

His mouth covered hers. He swallowed her startled gasp, then immediately deepened the contact. The tips of his fingers slipped into her hair, tangling in the strands while his lips and tongue continued their sensual, sweeping assault.

Sliding her hands up his muscled chest and around his neck, she held on for dear life. He insinuated a thigh between hers, and she shamelessly made room for him, welcoming the seductive pressure. His mouth slipped over hers, and his hands stroked her curves, molding her to him.

Kane tore his mouth from Megan's and buried his face against her neck. His ragged breathing blew hot and damp over her skin. "Oh, God, Megan," he gasped. "What are you doing to me?" His lips skimmed over her throat, followed by the soft caress of his tongue. "I want you so badly I ache constantly."

Plunging her fingers into his thick hair, she lifted his head to meet his gaze. For once, his barriers were down, his fear of falling for her evident in his beautiful, stormy eyes. "Then you know exactly how I feel."

"I don't want this." Trembling fingers gently touched her jaw, giving her a little more of the tenderness she knew he hid beneath layers of hurt. "*You* don't want this."

Grasping his hand before he could pull it away, she placed warm kisses on the tips of his fingers. "I do. More than anything."

He closed his eyes, a groan rumbling in his chest. "No. It won't work between us."

She could feel his caring, could feel him fighting the attraction. She nuzzled his palm, wanting to give him everything in her heart. "Maybe you're wrong."

His big body shuddered, but he managed to shake his head. "I'll only end up hurting you!"

Lifting her mouth to his, she nipped at his bottom lip, teasing and distracting him.

"Megan—"

"Shut up and kiss me, Kane."

He stared at her with dark eyes, denying himself what he wanted. She licked her bottom lip and arched slowly into him. "Kiss me again," she whispered.

With a low growl he did just that, a bottomless, soul-searching kiss brimming with emotion and a yearning so intense she could taste it. Maybe, just maybe, she thought, there was some feeling between them that could be nurtured into something stronger and infinitely more precious. If only he'd allow himself the chance.

His mouth left hers and charted a path to her earlobe. He caught the sensitive flesh between his teeth. His light stubble grazed her sensitive skin, and she shivered. His fingers worked on the buttons of her blouse, slowly undoing them. Cool air brushed across the upper slopes of her breasts, and her nipples tightened against the lacy webbing of her bra. He plucked at the sensitive tip through the sheer fabric until she had to bite her lip to keep from crying out.

A vague but logical part of her brain intruded on the moment, a cold dose of reality. "Kane... We can't do this. Not here."

"Megan..." His mouth moved to hers. "What am I going to do with you?" he asked between kisses.

Lord help her, she knew what she wanted him to do, but the sound of approaching footsteps instantly cleared any lingering fog clouding her good judgment. "Kane," she said, turning her head from his lips and pushing his shoulders. "We have to stop."

His mouth landed on her neck, and he nuzzled her. "Come to my room tonight."

She squirmed frantically, which only served to link their bodies more intimately. "We can't, Kane...please stop—"

"Oh, my goodness!"

A woman's shocked voice echoing from behind Kane accomplished what Megan hadn't been able to. Megan shook her head, wanting to apologize to him, but panic choked her. Kane straightened, the desire in his gaze eclipsed by apprehension and a gut-wrenching degree of dread. With a tenderness that made her heart ache, he pulled the sides of her blouse together and covered her decently before turning to face the woman standing just inside the barn. He was more concerned about her reputation than his own obvious arousal.

He brought his hands to hips and narrowed his gaze. With a resilience that amazed Megan, he composed himself into that cold, distant man.

Quickly buttoning her blouse, Megan shifted her gaze, looking over his shoulder to the woman. She was short and stocky, with graying brown hair and thick-rimmed glasses. One hand held a briefcase. Cradled in her other arm was a clipboard. Megan squinted at the identification tag pinned to her plain blue dress. The only words she could discern were Dept. of Human Services in big, bold type across the top of the tag. Megan held back a groan of dismay. The woman was a social worker!

"What can I do for you, Mrs. Henderson?" Kane asked, his voice so cold, Megan was surprised the woman didn't get frostbite.

Mrs. Henderson pursed her lips. She set her briefcase on the ground, then jotted a few notes on a piece of paper attached to her clipboard. "I was just following up on a complaint, but I can see for myself that we have a problem here."

"How do you figure? This is my home, and what I do here is my business."

The woman raised an incredulous brow. "Including consorting with females in the middle of the day with your son just outside this barn?"

As if realizing the implications of what they'd done, Kane swore vividly. "Did the Lindens send you?"

"That's confidential information," she said, lifting her chin haughtily.

Kane released a harsh breath. "Yeah, well, it wouldn't be the first time they've filed a complaint against me."

The woman looked from Kane to Megan, eyeing her with

a small degree of disdain. "Seems to me they had good reason."

Kane swore again and scrubbed a hand roughly over his jaw. Guilt weighed heavily on Megan. She'd been responsible for what had transpired, or at least she'd been the instigating party. If she hadn't challenged Kane and returned his kisses and caresses with such fervor, their escapade never would have gotten out of hand.

But it had, and they'd been caught. And if she didn't do something fast, Andrew would be the one to suffer the consequences.

She stepped next to Kane. He glared at her, tripling her guilt. He was furious, she knew. At her, himself and the situation. But beyond that green fire she witnessed fear and knew it was for Andrew's welfare.

Megan glanced at the social worker, willing to take all the blame in order to protect the two people who'd come to mean so much to her. "Mrs. Henderson, this isn't Kane's fault—"

"He seemed a willing party, Ms…?"

Megan flushed. "Megan. Megan Sanders," she said, watching as the woman made note of her name. "This isn't what it seems." Desperation laced her voice.

"Really?" The other woman scrutinized her with mocking curiosity. "Then maybe you'd like to explain what I saw?"

Suddenly, Megan realized how she must look after Kane's passionate assault. Her hair fell in wild tangles around her face and shoulders, and her lips still tingled from his thorough kiss.

Her stomach flipped, and she scrambled for a plausible excuse. "I…we…" No believable explanation sprang readily to mind.

"Megan, leave it alone." Kane's voice was strong, steady and sure, despite the hard edge to his jaw. "Why don't we go up to the house so we can discuss this?"

Mrs. Henderson nodded and picked up her briefcase.

"That would be a good start." Turning, she marched out of the barn.

With a long, resigned sigh, Kane started after her.

Megan grasped his sleeve, halting him. He met her gaze, and the worry shimmering there hit her like a fist to the midsection. What kind of penalty would he pay for their tryst, she wondered? Somehow, she knew it would be steep.

God, he probably hated her.

"Kane, surely that woman is only bluffing about the Lindens filing a complaint." The desperation in her voice was real.

A bitter smile twisted his lips. "Just like everyone else in this town, Mrs. Henderson is in the Lindens' pocket so deep—or rather, *Patricia's* pocket—that I wouldn't put it past Patricia to make sure Mrs. Henderson finds some kind of fault in this visit."

"Oh, Kane, I'm so sorry," she whispered, the words inadequate for the irreparable damage they might have done.

With a gentleness that made her heart ache, he brushed his knuckles across her smooth cheek. His eyes softened with regret, and a hint of a real smile touched his hard mouth. "So am I, Megan," he murmured. "So am I."

She watched him walk away, stunned at his display of tenderness and even more surprised that he didn't blame her. The knowledge nearly made her cry in relief. But there wasn't time, not with a social worker waiting to decide Andrew's fate.

She exited the barn in time to see Kane talking to Andrew. As she approached the pair she heard Kane tell his son that he had to take care of business with Mrs. Henderson and that he needed Andrew to play outside for a while. Andrew didn't look assured but obeyed his father.

In Kane's living room, Mrs. Henderson set her briefcase on the floor next to the recliner. She kept her clipboard in hand, staring at Megan in obvious disapproval. Before Megan could sit on the sofa, Kane's deep voice stopped her.

"Will you excuse us, Megan?"

Her first instinct was to protest. They'd both been a party to what happened in the barn, and if Mrs. Henderson's reprimand affected Andrew, she wanted to be involved. But one look at Kane's grim expression made her realize he had the most at stake and wanted to handle the situation alone.

Casting him an understanding look, she skirted the coffee table. "I'll go get us some refreshments."

She entered the kitchen and smacked herself on the forehead. "Refreshments, Megan?" she murmured as she sagged against the counter. "This is hardly a social call."

Needing something to keep her busy, she filled a tray with glasses, lemonade and cookies, which took all of three minutes. Impatient and restless, she paced the kitchen floor. Unable to stand another moment of confinement, she stood by the doorway connecting the two rooms and strained to hear the conversation drifting from the living room.

"Kane, Andrew needs to be in a stable environment, preferably with the guidance of two parents, not one who acts on frivolous desires," Mrs. Henderson said sternly. "It just isn't appropriate that you have a woman living with you—"

"Megan is *not* living with us," Kane replied, his voice tight with frustration.

"Regardless, it doesn't help matters that I've caught the two of you in a…well, a compromising position that is hardly conducive to Andrew's mental health." The woman sighed heavily. "I'm sorry, Kane, but I feel I have no other choice but to put in a recommendation that the Lindens receive temporary custody of Andrew until we can evaluate the situation further."

"I'll fight it," he said, his tone vibrating with anger.

Megan heard the sound of shuffling papers. "The report I'll be writing up and submitting today won't look good on your behalf."

"But I'm certain it'll look good on the Lindens' behalf," Kane added bitterly.

Megan clamped a hand over her mouth to stifle the sob

of despair working its way out of her throat. Tears burned her eyes, and the room began to spin.

Oh, Lord, what had she done?

Closing her eyes and bracing herself against the wall, she frantically searched her mind for something, *anything*, to remedy the awful predicament she'd gotten Kane into. She'd never forgive herself if she was the cause of tearing father and son apart, not to mention the resulting scandal that might hurt Andrew.

Then, like a godsend, an answer to their problem floated into her mind. Her solution was outrageous, but necessary to save Kane's reputation and keep Andrew where he belonged—with his father.

Not giving herself time to rethink her plan, she quickly picked up the tray of refreshments and strolled into the living room. Tension swirled between the adults. Kane looked at her, and the devastation and misery lining his pale face gave her the courage she needed to execute her plan.

Focusing all her hospitality on Mrs. Henderson, she placed the tray on the coffee table and sat next to Kane, so close that her thigh pressed against his. She didn't miss how he subtly shifted away so they weren't touching. "Has Kane had a chance to tell you our exciting news?"

The woman frowned and peered at her over her glasses. "What news is that?"

"Megan," Kane interrupted, his voice low with warning "I don't think Mrs. Henderson cares about *that* news."

He didn't want her help. Well, he didn't have a choice. "Oh, quit being so modest," she said sweetly as she poured lemonade into their glasses with a surprisingly steady hand. "You know everyone is going to find out sooner or later."

"*What* are you talking about?" Mrs. Henderson persisted.

She gave Kane a quick look that implored his trust before glancing at the social worker. "Well, Kane and I have been corresponding for a year and half, and he'd just asked me to marry him before you walked in on us. I've accepted his proposal."

The woman's brows rose so high they practically blended with her hairline. Skepticism shone in her eyes.

Ignoring her quivering insides, Megan smiled at Kane, who sat motionless beside her. The calm before the storm, she thought. The only clue belying his shock was his hands, fisted on his thighs, and the muscle ticking in his cheek.

"Isn't that right, honey?" Megan asked, knowing Mrs. Henderson would want him to confirm her claim.

His mouth thinned into a tight facsimile of a smile. Megan held her breath, waiting for Kane to either expose her lie or seal their future.

What seemed like an eternity passed. Then, as if finally realizing he had no other possible alternative if he didn't want to lose his son, the word wheezed out of him. "Yes."

Recovering, Mrs. Henderson softened her dour expression. Her face mellowed in approval. "Well, I honestly don't know what to say!"

Megan looped her arm through Kane's stiff one, knowing there'd be hell to pay once Mrs. Henderson left. It didn't matter, because she'd saved Kane and Andrew a ton of heartache.

Looking at her husband-to-be, she smiled adoringly. "How about congratulations?"

CHAPTER SIX

IMPOTENT fury raged through Kane. He expected steam to blow from his ears. He itched to plant his fist in something solid, to relieve some of the outrage simmering in him.

After making sure Mrs. Henderson had pulled her car out of the drive, he slammed the front door and charged into the living room. Megan stood at the window overlooking the front yard, arms crossed over her chest.

His temper came to a head and a violent trembling reverberated through his body. "What the hell do you think you're doing?"

She winced at his sharp tone and glanced at him. Her brilliant blue eyes were filled with a wealth of emotion, none of which resembled regret. "It was the only thing I could think of that would keep you and Andrew from being separated."

"Dammit, woman, I never asked you here, and I sure as hell don't need you meddling in my life!" He moved across the room toward her, his strides long and quick. Considering his furious tone and ominous expression, he was more than a little surprised she didn't scurry in the opposite direction. Instead, she stood her ground, that chin of hers lifting mutinously.

Scrubbing a hand through his hair, he released a harsh breath that eased some of the tension banding his chest. He knew she'd meant well, but... "For God's sake, Megan. *Marriage?* What in the world were you thinking?"

"She's not filing the complaint," she replied defensively.

"No, but that woman thinks we're getting married," he said, stabbing a finger in the direction Mrs. Henderson had followed less than five minutes ago. "In a matter of hours so will the rest of the town. Then what are we going to do?

Did you ever stop to think about the consequences of your brilliant plan?''

"Yes.''

"Really?'' he drawled, unable to help the dry, biting sarcasm in his voice. "And how do you propose we get out of this little predicament you've gotten us into without making both of us look like the liars we are?''

She drew a deep breath. "I know this is going to sound crazy, but maybe we should consider it.'' The words tumbled out in a rush of expelled air.

His stomach knotted with apprehension. "It?''

"Marriage,'' she clarified.

His heart slammed against his rib cage. The thought of sharing the kind of intimacy intrinsic to marriage made him break out in a cold sweat. "Not only is that a crazy idea, it's totally insane.''

She slowly approached him. "*I* don't think so.''

Her gaze never wavered from his, mesmerizing him. He couldn't recall ever knowing a woman so unselfish, so caring or generous. A woman more concerned about his and Andrew's welfare than her own. Her selfless sacrifice touched him deeply. He was a fool for pushing her away, for refusing something so sweet and tempting and infinitely precious, but he'd be a bigger fool if he allowed her to permanently insinuate herself in their lives. Megan would want to know all his secrets, would do her best to discover his biggest flaw. And when she did, he'd have to deal with her shock and her censure. He never wanted to see the softness in her blue eyes harden with resentment.

"Aw, Megan,'' he said, "I know what you're trying to do, and I appreciate the offer, but marriage isn't the answer.''

"How can you be so sure?'' she asked softly.

Her persistence both amused and irritated him. "Because I'm not husband material, and I don't want or need a wife.'' But Andrew *did* need a mother, and that thought buzzed around his conscience like a pesky gnat, forcing him to acknowledge everything Megan could offer his son.

"What will happen to Andrew if we don't get married?" she asked, her hands twisting anxiously at her waist. "Will Mrs. Henderson still give the Lindens temporary custody?"

Probably, he thought, unable to ignore the anger and bitterness the thought evoked. He moved to the living room window, braced a forearm on the casing and watched Andrew kick a soccer ball around on the front lawn. God, it would kill him to lose his son, the one person who made a difference in his life.

He sighed heavily. "Once you leave, I'll handle Mrs. Henderson, so don't worry about Andrew."

"How can I not?" she said, her voice rising in anger. "Kane, what happened this afternoon was my fault."

He glanced over his shoulder, giving her a halfhearted grin. "Like Mrs. Henderson said, I was a willing party."

"If Andrew becomes torn in a custody battle as a result of what happened, I'll never forgive myself." Tears welled in her eyes. "Especially if we have the ability to spare him that kind of heartache."

"Megan," he said softly and with more patience than God gave a saint, "marriage won't solve my problems with the Lindens." No, there was too much old hurt and blame between them. If anything, marriage to another woman would give the Lindens another reason to resent him.

"Maybe not completely, but they won't ever have any grounds to file for custody."

True, he thought, knowing that would be one advantage to being married. Andrew would have all the maternal influence he currently lacked. Another advantage would be a warm, willing wife in his bed, and a shared passion Kane knew he'd never tire of. Desire stirred within him at the image of making love with Megan, of burying himself so deeply in her body that he forgot all the differences that separated them.

But in the light of dawn, reality had a nasty habit of putting everything into its proper perspective. Their differences were vast and very complicated. His guard would have to remain intact to protect his pride. He would have to keep his emotions withdrawn.

She was willing to sacrifice so much, and he had nothing substantial to offer her in exchange. His simple way of life couldn't much compare to her life in Seattle.

That thought brought to mind an interesting question. "You have a life in Seattle. Why are you so willing to give it up for a small town like Linden? There's nothing for you here."

"Andrew is here," she said simply.

He shook his head in amazement, baffled at how one little boy could mean so much to her that she'd relocate without a moment's pause. "But your life is in Seattle."

She gave a short laugh that held more sadness than humor. "My *life* consists of a shared apartment, a few friends and a career that can relocate as easily as I can."

"I just don't get it, Megan. There are plenty of beneficial reasons for *me* to marry *you,* especially where Andrew is concerned, but what's in this for you?"

Her mood suddenly turned somber. "The chance to raise a child."

He frowned, not understanding her logic. "You don't need marriage for that."

"No, not in this modern age of single parenting and artificial insemination," she agreed wryly. "But I don't want to be a single parent, and artificial insemination sounds like such a cold process. What I want, what I've wanted since I was a young girl, is a family, and that's what you, Andrew and I can be."

She made it sound so easy. Too easy. "How come you didn't have a family with your ex-husband?"

"Because he didn't want one."

"That's why you're divorced?" he said, guessing.

"Yes. He decided his career in the legal field was more important than having a family, and having a family was too important to me to stay in a childless marriage." Moving to the couch, she held his gaze steadily, sincerely. "I love the kind of warmth and closeness I share with

Andrew, especially since I never had that as a child growing up in foster homes. I know this might sound silly to
you, but after years of feeling so out of place, I've finally
found a place where I feel like I belong.''

"In Linden?'' His voice was incredulous.

A small smile touched her mouth. ''I never did like the
city, but that's where I was raised and that's where my ex-
husband wanted to stay. It's so clear and beautiful here,
and such a different way of life. Slow. Unencumbered.
Wholesome.''

"Try living here your whole life,'' he said cynically.

Her expression turned soft and wistful. ''I wish I had.''

Their gazes holding, something connected between them.
If she'd grown up in Linden, would they have been friends?
Or would she have kept her distance like most of the other
women? Would he have married Cathy, or would he have
fallen hard for Megan and her warm, accepting ways? He
couldn't help but think how different their lives might have
turned out if they'd known one another...couldn't stop the
image of her round with his child, excited about the pros-
pect of having a baby. *His* baby.

"Now that I've bared everything about myself,'' Megan
said, ''you know why I wouldn't hesitate to marry you,
move out of state and be with Andrew. I love him very
much, and you know I care for you.''

But was that enough? ''I know you do, but—''

"It can be a marriage of convenience,'' she suggested in
a rush, as if sensing a rejection. ''Andrew needs a maternal
influence, and I can provide that. I don't mind cooking and
cleaning and taking care of the house. I can set up a desk
over in that corner and write my books here at home and
still be here for Andrew on a daily basis.'' She worried her
bottom lip, her gaze bright with silent invocation. ''Kane,
I don't have any motives other than just wanting to be with
Andrew. And I don't want him to be torn between you and
the Lindens.''

He believed her, had seen her with Andrew and knew
she'd never deliberately hurt him. She made the whole

package sound so appealing, but something dark and deeply buried rebelled, reminding him of another woman's promises…and her ultimate rejection.

Apprehension closed in on him, clouding his judgment. "I don't know, Megan," he said, staring at his hands, clasped between his spread thighs. "I never planned on marrying again."

"I understand," she said quietly, though there was enough optimism in her voice to make Kane realize that she *didn't* understand his reluctance, or his fears. "But please think about my proposition…for Andrew's sake."

Megan watched the large, shadowy figure approach the house. She knew it was Kane finally returning from wherever he'd disappeared to after dinner. Her heart skipped a beat, and her fingers curled around the chain holding up the porch swing.

Had he come to a decision? For the rest of the afternoon and early evening she'd replayed their conversation in her mind. And with her realization that living in Linden and helping to raise Andrew was what she wanted came the acceptance that she was in love with Kane.

The emotion had crept up on her, slowly taking residence in her heart right next to the love she harbored for Andrew. Being in love with Kane was both a frightening and exciting experience, much like being on a nonstop roller coaster. A small smile touched her lips. No doubt life with Kane would be just that, a wild, reckless ride full of dips, turns and surprises.

He shuffled up the steps, and when the light swept over his face, she saw the day's accumulation of weariness reflected in his eyes. He'd obviously struggled to come to a decision, and she silently prayed he'd realized how much they could offer one another.

He sat on the opposite end of the swing, his weight causing the wood to creak. "Where's Andrew?" he asked, casting a quick glance through the screen door.

"Taking a bath."

"Good." His gaze met hers, dark and stormy with reluctant acquiescence. "Andrew is the most important thing in my life, and I don't want to lose him, and I don't want him to be torn between a custody battle between me and his grandparents."

"I don't, either," she said softly.

He rubbed his palms down the denim encasing his thighs. "I've decided to accept your proposal."

"I'm glad," she said evenly, suppressing the impulse to throw her arms around his neck and express her gratitude with a kiss for the precious gift he was giving her.

He slanted her a wry look. "Yeah, well, before you sacrifice yourself at the altar, there's a few things I want you to know up front."

"Okay." She waited for the first bombshell to drop.

"I'm not in love with you, and I doubt I ever could be."

She saw past his statement to his subconscious ploy. He was trying to secure those walls of his, erecting them like a steel fortress around his heart. *Don't bother, Kane. I'm gonna spend every day of our married years together proving you wrong.*

"Do you care about me?" she asked, tilting her head curiously.

A startled look passed over his features, immediately masked by a frown. "Yes, but don't mistake it for love."

She dismissed the warning in his words. Caring was a good enough start for her. "What else do you want me to know?"

"I'm no good at being married," he said gruffly. "I already told you how disastrous my first marriage was."

She glanced at her lap to conceal her smile. She was quickly learning that Kane tried to intimidate her whenever he was feeling vulnerable or threatened. She took it as a positive sign. "I'll take my chances. What else?"

"The town has their own opinion of me, and my in-laws can't stand me." He rested his arm along the back of the swing, stretching his shirt taut across his chest. "By default of marriage, you'll have to put up with your share of conjecture.''

In time, she hoped to remedy the situation with the Lindens. "I already told you I can handle the town's speculation. As for your in-laws, be grateful you only have one set to put up with." She pushed the swing into action with the toe of her shoe. "Anything else I need to know?''

"I prefer being alone." His tone was low but lacked the harshness he would have displayed less than a week ago.

"I don't believe that."

"Okay, the nights get cold and lonely," he admitted, a brief, rakish smile lifting his lips. "Which brings me around to my next stipulation."

"Which is?''

He fingered a strand of hair near the side of her neck, then gently tucked it behind her ear. "A marriage of convenience is out of the question."

Her pulse tripped all over itself, and she dampened her suddenly dry lips with her tongue. "Meaning?"

His fingers fluttered along her neck to the pulse thrumming at the base of her throat. The soft, butterfly caress made her nerve endings tingle and the tips of her breasts tighten. He must have noticed her soft catch of breath, because his gaze darkened with a sensual hunger that matched her own.

"Meaning?" she prompted again, her voice husky.

"Meaning, you sleep in my bed, every night, and I want my husbandly rights."

Those wonderful fingers of his continued their light, provocative dance up the side of her neck, making her shiver and nearly groan.

He smiled. "I want you, Megan. Considering the way you respond to my touch, I believe the feeling is mutual."

Oh, it was, and her body was responding in ways that made her ache for a more intimate contact than the two feet separating them allowed. There was no way she'd refuse something she wanted so badly. He made her hot and restless, and feel more desirable than she had in years.

"Are you agreeable with my terms?"

She nodded, not trusting herself to speak.

"Any stipulations of your own?"

Only that you trust me, and in time learn to love me. She tucked her coveted wish away, knowing he wasn't ready to hear something so forthright. "Only one."

He arched a dark brow. "You want your wifely rights?"

Sensing him relaxing and growing comfortable with her, she took a gamble. "Kane, I don't want any lies or secrets between us."

His body visibly tensed. Dark shadows passed over his features, drawing him into his protective shell where no one could trespass. "Everyone has secrets," he said roughly.

"And I shared mine with you, about my divorce and my past."

His bitter laughter grated on her nerves. "You know that I killed my wife."

She didn't bother correcting him. "I think there's more."

As if she'd crossed a fine line, he narrowed his gaze. His eyes flared with emerald heat. He leaned toward her, his lips curling into a feral smile that should have sent her bolting into the house. It would have, if he hadn't reminded her of a wounded animal trying to ward off an enemy. But she wasn't the enemy, and that thought kept her rooted to her seat.

"They call them secrets for a reason, Megan—because they're better left buried," he said, his voice harsh.

"And sometimes you have to trust someone enough to share them."

"Trust *me*, Megan. There are things about me you don't want to know. Just remember that, and we'll get along fine." He abruptly stood, ending the conversation. "If it's convenient for you, I'll make an appointment on Friday with Judge Griffen for a civil ceremony."

She looked at him. Her heart sank at his grim expression. This certainly wasn't the romantic proposal of her first marriage, but then Phillip hadn't turned out to be the prince of her dreams, either, she reminded herself. "That'll be fine. I'll start settling my affairs in Seattle."

He nodded curtly and opened the door, but paused on the threshold to glance at her. "Be sure about your decision, Megan," he said in a flat tone. "Divorce isn't something I'll consider in the future."

He walked into the house, leaving her feeling cold and lonely but not regretting her resolution to remain in Linden as Kane's wife and Andrew's new mother. Life and time, she'd learned, had a way of working out all the rough spots.

"I can't believe you talked me into this," Kane muttered as they walked up the cobblestone walkway to the Lindens' elegant two-story Victorian home.

Megan smothered a smile. Kane would never admit it, but she knew he was nervous about attending the annual birthday party the Lindens threw in Andrew's honor, especially since the Lindens didn't know they were coming.

"If we're going to be a family, we need to start acting like one." Switching Andrew's birthday present to her other arm, she hooked her hand through Kane's elbow and gave him a light squeeze that did nothing to ease his rigid posture. "So smile and try to make the best of it."

He glowered at her, trying to hide the dread in his gaze. It seemed to increase the closer they came to the Lindens' front door. "Kinda hard to do when I'd rather be anywhere but here."

She didn't doubt that, but if Kane didn't already realize it, she was relentless when it came to something she believed in. And more than anything, she wanted Kane and the Lindens to put the past aside and reconcile. "Look how happy you've made Andrew."

Kane's expression softened as he watched Andrew skip ahead of them. Since learning that morning before going to school that his father and Megan planned to get married, he'd been blissfully happy. After a boisterous "Yippee!", he'd skipped around the living room proclaiming, "This is the best birthday present ever!"

Megan's heart swelled at the memory, and at the warm way Kane had smiled at her. And for one perfect moment, she believed he truly could love her.

"Hurry up, Megan and Dad!" Andrew waited at the double oak doors with etched glass insets, fidgeting impatiently.

Megan grinned. "Don't worry, the party can't start without you."

As soon as they climbed the porch stairs, Andrew flung open the front door without knocking and rushed inside. "Guess what, everyone!" he shouted gleefully.

As they stepped in, Megan kept a firm hold on Kane's arm so he couldn't retreat at the last moment. The house was packed with adults and children. Balloons and streamers decorated the entryway, and in the adjoining living room a clown was busy entertaining the kids with magic tricks.

Patricia Linden smiled at her grandson, unaware of the extra guests who'd arrived. "What is it, Andrew?" she asked, fussing unnecessarily with the collar of his shirt.

Excitement wreathed Andrew's face. "Megan and my dad are getting married!"

Megan cringed, and the muscles in Kane's forearm twitched, the only indication of his unease. Andrew's broadcast caused a hush to fall over the general area. The adults standing nearby stopped their conversations to stare. They didn't seem surprised, merely curious, which confirmed Kane's claim that Mrs. Henderson would spread the news.

Patricia straightened and finally looked beyond Andrew. Her mouth pursed into a thin line of displeasure. "So we've heard."

Smiling despite the uncomfortable atmosphere, Megan moved forward, propelling a stiff and reluctant Kane with her. She figured the only way she'd beat Patricia at her own game was to overwhelm her with kindness. Since Kane wasn't inclined to be hospitable, it would be up to her to extend the first greeting.

"Hello, Patricia." She gave the other woman Andrew's present, a subtle gesture to let her know they planned to stay for the festivities. "What a lovely home you have."

"Thank you," she said stiffly, then turned and headed into the next room, calling over her shoulder, "Come along, Andrew, your guests are waiting."

Nobody went out of their way to welcome them. She saw Harold, and although he gave her a slight smile and a nod of acknowledgment, he made no move to approach them, nor did Kane make any attempt to be friendly, either. It was as if Patricia had set the precedence for her guest's behavior around her and Kane.

Frustrated with everyone's attitude, Megan left Kane talking to Gus—a foreman at the sawmill and apparently the only one brave enough to risk Patricia's wrath—and went in search of something to drink. Stubborn people, she thought, wondering what it would take to get the town to accept Kane.

A lavish catered dinner of salads, chicken and ribs covered a long picnic table in the landscaped back yard. She poured herself a cup of punch from a large cooler, took a sip and watched Andrew and his friends take turns hitting a piñata filled with treats.

"This is a first," a throaty female voice said.

Megan turned to see Joyce, who must have just arrived. Megan counted the young woman as an ally admist all the discord, despite her penchant for spreading rumors. "What's a first?"

"Kane coming to Andrew's party." Joyce dipped a carrot stick into ranch dressing and crunch into the vegetable. "You must be quite an influence."

It had been like pulling teeth. "He wanted to be here," she said, taking another sip of punch while making a mental note to talk to Kane about Joyce not tutoring Andrew once they were married.

"Umm." Joyce dipped her carrot again, a sly smile lifting her lips. "I hear congratulations are in order."

Had Mrs. Henderson posted the news of their pending

nuptuals in the *Daily Register*? "Yes, thank you. Kane and I are getting married tomorrow."

Corey, Andrew's best friend, split open the piñata, and the kids squealed in delight. Candy dropped to the ground, and they scrambled after it. Megan smiled at the scene, thinking next year they'd have Andrew's birthday party at *their* house, and the Lindens would attend. Willingly, she hoped.

"I don't know how you did it, but it looks like you landed quite a catch," Joyce said, interrupting Megan's thoughts.

"Yes, I did," she said, meaning it. Over Joyce's shoulder, Megan watched Kane walk toward them, looking cool and standoffish. How did he expect to win over these people when his body language said back off? He stopped next to her, and she offered him a smile he didn't return.

"Hello, Joyce," he said brusquely.

"Hi, Kane," she said, ducking her head guiltily. She waved at a young blond man across the yard and started to back away, seemingly anxious to go. "Well, good luck to the both of you."

Kane frowned after her. "What was that all about?"

Megan finished her punch and tossed the paper cup into the trash. "Joyce just wanted to offer her congratulations."

A tight smile creased his lips. "How...sweet."

Tired of his unreceptive behavior, she gave him a pointed look. "You know, Kane, if you insist on keeping everyone at a distance, they're going to have nothing to go on but their own speculation." She leaned close and pressed a hand to his chest, deliberately giving everyone watching them the impression that they were intimate. His heartbeat quickened beneath her palm, granting her a small measure of feminine satisfaction. "I know you're not the man they think you are, but you have to make the effort to prove it to them."

He covered her hand with his, stroking the sensitive skin connecting each of her fingers. Instant heat spiraled through

her body, contradicting the chilling intensity of his gaze.
"I don't need to prove anything to anyone."

Of course he didn't, she thought unkindly. His bitterness
about the past got in the way of his pride. With a sigh, she
let the subject drop.

Patricia announced it was time to cut the cake, then open
presents. Megan dragged Kane to a crowd of people gathered around Andrew. They wove their way to the table so
they could stand next to the birthday boy. All eyes were
on them.

Kane shifted uncomfortably as they sang Happy Birthday
to Andrew, who beamed at them with a dimpled grin. As
soon as the song was over, Kane slipped away, preferring
to sit by himself rather than stand in line with Megan for
a piece of cake.

After giving Andrew a big birthday hug, Megan picked
up two slices of cake. On her way to Kane, she saw Patricia
standing alone at the picnic table and approached her, forcing down the sudden knot of nervousness forming in her
throat.

"Patricia?"

The older woman turned and saw Megan. Undisguised
hostility flared in her pale blue eyes. "I don't believe we
have anything to say to one another." She continued to
cover salads with plastic wrap.

Megan wasn't discouraged. "Maybe you don't think so,
but I'd like to thank you for giving Andrew such a special
birthday party."

Patricia straightened and leveled her gaze at Megan.
"He's my grandchild," she said in a low voice. "My *only*
grandchild, and I'd do *anything* to be sure he has everything
he might want or need."

Megan's fingers clenched on the paper plates in her
hands as she attempted to keep her rising ire at bay. "Kane
is a good father, and Andrew certainly doesn't lack for
anything."

Patricia slanted a cold glare in Kane's direction. "Except

maybe his *real* mother.'' She obviously placed the blame on her son-in-law's shoulders.

Megan managed to maintain her composure by sheer force of will. Anger wouldn't bridge the chasm between families, just inflate it. ''Patricia, I'm sorry about the loss of your daughter, but I'd like to think we could be friends. Especially since I'll be part of the family.''

''Part of the family?'' She looked down her nose at Megan. ''If you think you can replace Cathy—''

''I'm not trying to replace her,'' she cut in, appalled that anyone would think that was her intent. And then she caught a brief glimpse of sadness and pain in Patricia's eyes and knew Patricia wasn't ready to give up her daughter's memory to a stranger, felt threatened that Andrew would forget any wispy recollection he might have of his real mother as a result of Kane marrying her.

Megan's heart went out to Patricia, and she searched for a way to offer her a little peace of mind. ''I care for Andrew a great deal, and although I would like to be his mother in an emotional way, he will *never* forget who his real mother is.''

''I'll be sure of that,'' Patricia said coldly. Picking up the potato salad, she marched past Megan with her head held high.

Feeling mild defeat, Megan headed to Kane, grateful that a shade tree had kept him from witnessing her exchange with Patricia. No sense upsetting both parties, she thought wryly.

''I brought you a piece of cake,'' she said, bribing him with a slice.

He took a plate and picked at the butter-cream frosting with his fork. ''Don't you think we've overstayed our welcome?''

After my run-in with Patricia, definitely, she mused. But she couldn't let one unpleasant encounter deter her from her goal. ''Nope. Andrew's opening his presents as we speak. Or should I say tearing into them.'' She glanced at her watch. ''Another hour ought to do it.''

Kane groaned. "I could be home in an hour if I walked."

"Megan!" Andrew shouted, barreling toward them with the book she'd written for him in his hands. "I love my new book about the tooth fairy."

She smiled. "I'm glad. Maybe we can get your dad to read it to you," she said, remembering Kane's tale about his tooth fairy blunder, the basis of the book.

The pure panic reflected in Kane's face puzzled her, as did his paling complexion. "I, uh, I don't think—"

"Dad says I'm too old to have books read to me," Andrew cut in, hanging his head and scuffing his sneaker in the grass. "But every once in a while he lets me read one to him, just to make sure I'm keeping up on my reading level."

Just like he insisted on Andrew having a tutor who made sure he brushed up on his reading skills. Megan wondered why Kane thought it so important, but she knew now was not the time to press the issue. "Then you can read the story to both of us."

"Okay." Seemingly content with that idea, Andrew grinned and glanced at Kane. "So, are you having fun, Dad?" His voice rose a level, and he clutched the book to his chest, waiting for his dad's approval.

Kane hesitated, looking beyond his son to all the people who should have been friends but were merely acquaintances. Megan nudged Kane in the side with her elbow. Hard.

After shooting her a quick, disgruntled look, Kane smiled at Andrew, obeying Megan's silent prompting. "Yeah, sport, I'm having a great time."

"*Married?* Are you out of your mind?"

Megan cringed and pulled the receiver away from her ear as her best friend's high-pitched voice traveled over the phone lines. "I'm perfectly sane, Judi."

"Cripes, Megan, you hardly know this guy."

Megan wrapped the phone cord around her wrist and leaned against the kitchen wall. She'd thought she'd known

Phillip, and look where that had gotten her. "Kane's a good man, and you know how I feel about Andrew."

"Yeah, I do," Judi said, her voice soft with understanding.

She explained what had happened with Mrs. Henderson, and how Kane's in-laws wouldn't hesitate to file for custody after they'd been caught in such a compromising position. "I…I love Kane," she admitted, "and I know he at least cares for me. He's giving me the opportunity to raise a child I love with all my heart."

"Megan," Judi said, sounding exasperated. "This just isn't like you to do something so…"

"Spontaneous?"

"Crazy was the word I was looking for."

Megan laughed. "I'm not crazy. For once in my life I finally feel like I've found a place I belong. I love it here in Linden. No crowds, no hassles, just the kind of simple life-style I've always yearned for. And now I'll have a family, too."

"Then I'm happy for you, but I'm going to miss you," Judi said, her sentiment genuine. "What do you want me to do with your stuff?"

She was going to miss Judi, too. They'd shared so much, but she was confident a strong friendship like theirs would remain constant. "You can keep all the furniture in the apartment." Most of it had been hers, from her marriage to Phillip. Furniture and fixtures that had no sentimental value. She much preferred Kane's handcrafted things and down-home furnishings. "If you don't mind, could you ship my personal items and writing supplies overnight air?"

"No problem. I'll have them out by tomorrow."

They spent another half hour on the phone, talking about the past and what the future might hold for both of them. Tears filled Megan's eyes when it came time for them to hang up.

"Megan, be sure that this is what you truly want," Judi

said, always the friend who tried to protect Megan from heartbreak.

Megan smiled while wiping a sentimental tear from her cheek. Judi had nothing to worry about. "I've never been so sure of anything in all my life."

CHAPTER SEVEN

"BY THE power vested in me, I now pronounce you husband and wife." Judge Griffen smiled at the small gathering of people in his private chambers. "You may kiss your bride."

Kane turned and looked at the woman standing by his side. *His wife.* The title sent a warmth rippling through him, filling him with a possessiveness he hadn't expected. The sensation wasn't all that unpleasant.

Dressed in a simple cream suit, her auburn hair swept into a fancy twist at the back of her head, Megan exemplified a bride in every sense of the word. She looked radiant and beautiful. Joy shone in her drown-in-them-forever blue eyes, and a deeper emotion he didn't take time to analyze. A pink blush colored her cheeks. In her right hand she clutched the small bouquet of flowers Andy had insisted he buy for her. The pale pink baby roses and tiny white flowers trembled with every breath she took.

He still held her left hand, where he'd placed a simple gold wedding band. The ring had been his mother's. No diamonds or expensive frills. He was determined to begin this marriage as practically as the reasons that had brought them together.

"Dad, he said you can kiss her," Andy whispered from behind them, his small voice exasperated.

Jeff, who'd stood in as Kane's best man and a witness to the ceremony, chuckled. "Yeah, Fielding, we're waiting."

Megan laughed nervously, and Kane shot his friend a not-so-subtle look before returning his gaze to Megan. God, how was he ever going to live up to the expectation shimmering in her eyes?

Pushing his doubts aside, he brushed his mouth across

103

hers, a quick, fleeting kiss that only whet his appetite for more. Her lips parted, damp and inviting, but he pulled away, knowing one taste wouldn't be enough.

"Yeah, Dad, you did it!" Andy said, giving Corey and Tanner a high five. Rushing around Jeff, he gave Kane and Megan a joyful hug that left everyone laughing. Once the embrace ended, he danced around the judge's chamber singing, "I got a new mom, I got a new mom!"

Grinning at Andrew's enthusiasm, Megan signed the marriage certificate, then passed the pen to Kane. After a brief hesitation, he wrote his name next to hers, an illegible scrawl that had become his signature over the years.

"Congratulations, Kane," Jeff said, clapping Kane on the back in masculine camaraderie. "Didn't think you'd ever tie the knot again."

Neither did I, Kane thought, returning Jeff's handshake.

Karen gave Kane an appraising look before placing a sisterly kiss on his cheek. "I knew something was going on between the two of you." Turning, she gave Megan a friendly hug, welcoming her into the fold. "The both of you look very happy together."

Kane *was* happy, he realized, and refused to fight the feeling on his wedding day. What harm was there in enjoying Andrew's delight, the company of his only true friends and the way Megan tentatively slipped her hand through his arm and gazed at him with a reverence that nearly stole his breath. Damn, he thought, looking away. He wasn't worthy of such unconditional devotion.

"Come on, everyone," Jeff announced, herding them toward the chamber's double panel doors. "The wedding dinner is on me."

A half an hour later the group sat in a large booth at Callahan's, the finest steak house in Linden. After a cursory glance at the menu, Kane ordered the porterhouse steak specialty the waiter had recommended. Once everyone else had ordered, Jeff requested a bottle of expensive wine and sodas for the kids.

"I'd like to make a toast," Jeff proposed, pouring each

of the adults a glass of wine. He raised his glass, and everyone followed suit. "To Kane and Megan. May your love
endure good and bad times."

"Here, here!" Karen clinked her glass to Megan's and
Kane's, starting a chain reaction around the table that ended
with gales of laughter from the boys.

After dinner, Jeff and Karen took Andrew home with
them for the weekend, explaining to him that Megan and
Kane needed time alone to get acquainted. Without
Andrew's incessant chatter, the drive home was strangely
quiet, but an undercurrent of sexual tension hummed between them. They both knew what would happen tonight…the beginning of their honeymoon.

Jeff had insisted that Kane take the next week off and
go somewhere with his new bride, but the thought of being
alone with Megan for seven days, with nowhere to escape
if he needed to, kept Kane from accepting his boss's generous offer. At home, at least, he was free to come and go
if the events of the past week suddenly overwhelmed him
or if the thought of the future sent him into a panicked
state.

Keeping his gaze trained on the beam of headlights illuminating the road, he turned into his dirt drive and parked
the car near the house. Silently, they exited the car and
walked toward the porch. Moonlight glittered off a silver
ice bucket perched on the porch railing, the neck of a champagne bottle sticking from the rim.

"Looks like the word has spread," Kane said in a wry
tone. He unlocked the front door, flipped on the porch light
and came up behind Megan, thrusting his hands deep in his
pants pockets. A light evening breeze blew, carrying the
feminine, floral scent of his wife. He resisted the urge to
bury his face in the fragrant hollow of her neck and forget
about the impromptu wedding gift sitting on his porch.

"There's a card," she said, picking up the small white
envelope propped against the bucket. "Let's see who it's
from."

He'd seen the envelope, but he hadn't been about to

touch it. But he was curious as hell who'd signed it. "By all means, let's."

"You don't have to be so flippant about it." She slipped a manicured nail beneath the flap while giving him a chastising look, tempered by something soft and infinitely sexy.

He pulled on the knot of his tie, loosening it from around his neck. "I just can't imagine anyone in this town going out of their way to congratulate us."

She frowned as she quietly read the message. "Well, whoever it is, they want to remain anonymous." She flipped the card toward him.

Kane's heart leaped into his throat. He stared at the bold script on the small card with wedding bells adorning one corner. Pure panic swamped him. She gave him a peculiar look, and he knew he had to think fast or sink even faster. "I have horrible night vision," he said abruptly, squinting at the card. "What does it say?"

Her puzzled expression faded, replaced by a dramatic sigh. "Congratulations and best wishes—a friend," she recited breezily, then stuffed the card into the envelope. Turning, she patted his cheek and grinned sassily. "Your sparkling conversation at Andrew's birthday party must have won over a few people."

He wanted to laugh in relief and frustration. Instead, he gently grabbed her wrist, willing away the awful, sickening feeling churning in the pit of his stomach. Rubbing his thumb over the pulse in her wrist, he intentionally gave her something other than that damned card, and his reaction to it, to think about. "Regardless of who sent the champagne, I plan on enjoying it."

Her lashes fell to half-mast. "Sounds good to me," she said, her voice throaty.

Reluctantly, he released her. He picked up the ice bucket in one arm, opened the door for her with his free hand, then followed her inside the dark house. He set the champagne on the coffee table, switched on a lamp and shucked his coat and tie. He popped free the first three buttons on his shirt to give him some breathing room.

While he wrestled the plastic cork from the bottle, Megan turned on the stereo to a mellow station playing ballads, adjusting the volume to fill the sudden awkward silence between them.

This was their wedding night, and even though they both knew what the result would be, he didn't want to rush through the preliminaries leading up to their lovemaking. They had all evening, all weekend, and he wanted to fill himself with every nuance of Megan, savor everything about his wife.

He had no fancy champagne flutes, so he retrieved two glasses from the kitchen and filled them with the bubbly drink. He handed one to her and they clinked them together in a silent toast and drank deeply. Powerless to keep his hands to himself any longer, he took Megan's glass from her and set the pair next to the ice bucket.

"Isn't it a tradition that the groom gets to dance with his bride?" he asked, drawing her into his arms without any protest from her. He didn't claim to be Fred Astaire. He just wanted to hold her, touch her, drown in the light, floral scent of her. In other words, he wanted to drive himself crazy, and dancing close seemed like a damned good start in accomplishing his goal.

Her lithe body flowed into him. She tucked one hand in his and wrapped the other around his neck, a tremulous smile on her lips. "This hasn't been a very traditional wedding."

"Depends on whose tradition."

She laughed throatily and curled tighter against him. "We're making our own?"

"We could." He smoothed a strand of hair from her flushed cheek, curbing the impulse to pull the pins out of her hair and sift his fingers through the silky mass. Soon, he thought. "We've got a lot of years ahead of us. We should make the best of it."

Her beautiful smile fell away, and her lashes swept downward in an attempt to hide her emotions. But he knew she was thinking about their conversation about keeping secrets. God, he could give her anything but the truth, a shocking revelation that could easily tear apart the fragile vows that bound them. Coward or not, he wouldn't make the same mistake twice.

Wanting her to forget everything but them, he swept a hand down her back, ran that same hand over her bottom and squeezed. Her breath hitched in her throat and her eyes flew open, wide with arousal. Her soft sigh rolled into a quiet groan of need. In an instant he was hard and aching.

Tipping her chin up with his thumb and forefinger, he lowered his head and captured her parted lips in a deep, openmouthed kiss that she returned fervently. Her fingers slid into the hair at the nape of his neck, and she clung to him. A raging need pounded through him, threatening the tight rein on his control. With effort, he ended the kiss and set her away from him.

They both gasped for breath, but he managed to catch his long enough to say, "If we don't stop now, we'll be on that couch making love with half our clothes still on."

Looking dazed, Megan dragged her tongue over her bottom lip, still damp and swollen from his kiss. He suppressed a groan and the urge to follow through with his threat.

"Megan," he warned thickly.

She smiled at him, a vixen smile that beckoned and cajoled. "I...I think I'll go change," she whispered.

Her sultry invitation was clear, but he didn't follow her into his bedroom, opting instead to give her some time alone to prepare for their wedding night.

Half an hour and two glasses of champagne later, he entered his bedroom. The lights were off, but the room glowed from the five candles she'd lit and placed on the nightstand and dresser, giving the room a romantic ambience. The sweet scent of vanilla permeated the air, swirling around his senses like a potent aphrodisiac.

She'd turned down the bed, the bedspread folded neatly at the end of the mattress and crisp sheets pulled aside. Already she'd made her mark on his bedroom, having moved her clothes and personal belongings there that morning.

He heard a sound behind him and turned. His mouth went as dry as dust as he stared at the apparition in front of him. Nothing in his wildest fantasies came close to setting his blood on fire as the sight that greeted him.

This was no fantasy. Megan was a flesh-and-blood woman, sexy, sensual and tempting. She wore a silky peach nightie that reached mid-thigh, the flowing hem flirting enticingly as she shifted on bare feet. He dragged his gaze up, over the shadowed valley at the juncture of her thighs to where sheer lace cupped and molded her breasts.

Her hair spilled around her shoulders and shimmered like burnished gold in the candlelight. He nearly groaned at the sweet promises in her gaze. In that moment he selfishly wanted to take everything she was willing to give. And he hated himself because he had nothing to give her in return. His heart was empty, his soul too full of dark secrets to ever be redeemed.

But tonight he didn't want to disappoint her. Tonight he'd be everything she wanted him to be, if only for a few hours.

"C'mere," he murmured.

She moved forward, a hint of vulnerability passing over her features, and stopped an arm's length away. "I was beginning to wonder if you'd changed your mind."

Not a chance, sweetheart. "I took our wedding vows seriously, and I meant what I said about a divorce. Until death us do part."

Her head tilted. "I mean about a marriage of convenience."

He laughed and slowly circled her. "I'm just a man, Megan. And like any man, I want my wife."

Standing behind her, he cupped her smooth shoulders in his palms and turned her so she could see their reflections in the dresser mirror. He slid his hands down her arms and grasped her hips, tucking her bottom against the ridged length confined behind the zipper of his slacks. He heard her soft indrawn breath, and a smile tugged his lips.

"Nervous?" he asked, his mouth skimming her ear.

"A little." She shivered and rested her head on his shoulder, her back arching when his palms moved over the silk covering her belly. His warm, searching hands stopped just beneath the slope of her breasts, his fingers spreading wide over her rib cage.

Her breathing deepened. "It's been a long time."

"Yeah, for me, too," he admitted. Nuzzling her neck, he continued to explore the dips and curves of her body through silk, deliberately avoiding all the places he knew ached for his touch.

"I'm hardly a virgin," she said breathlessly, her eyes wide and unfocused in the mirror. "But, well, it still feels like it's my first time."

"It is your first time," he said, turning her to face him. "With me."

"Yes." Reaching for his hand, she pressed a damp kiss in the center, then leisurely dragged his palm down her throat. Her needy, unguarded gaze burned him to his soul. Brazenly, she pressed his hand to the full, taut swell of her breast.

His fingers flexed around the soft mound of flesh, and her nipple hardened. "I'm yours, Kane," she whispered, candlelight and emotion softening her gaze. "Any time you want me."

His heart gave a crazy little leap. "That's quite an invitation."

She stared deep into his eyes. "As your wife, I'll do whatever I can to make you happy."

Lifting his hand from her breast, he rubbed the coarse pad of his thumb across her bottom lip. "Anything?" The possibilities of such a generous overture aroused more than his interest.

An intoxicating combination of trust and desire welled within the bottomless depths of her eyes. "Yes."

"Take the nightgown off for me. Slowly."

The shock he'd been expecting never materialized. Instead, his wife surprised him with her sassy, very husky comeback. "I wore it for you. *You* take it off."

He chuckled ruefully. Megan would never be one of those meek, docile wives who obeyed a husband's orders. No, her candid, no-holds-barred attitude was the reason they were married—she was strong-spirited, determined and damned sexy while doing it. In some ways her straightforward approach scared the hell out of him. Now, alone in his bedroom, it excited him beyond his wildest dreams.

Wanting to beat her at her sensual game, he lifted her hands and placed them on his chest. Her touch singed him even through the cotton of his shirt, and his heart responded with a distinct thump beneath her palm. She looked at him, questioning eyes filled with heat and undisguised passion.

Knowing once he removed that flimsy gown he wouldn't be able to maintain his control, he brought her fingers to the buttons on his shirt. "I'll take your nightgown off after *you* undress *me*."

Her mouth curled in a smile so full of seduction he knew he was in trouble no matter who undressed who first.

Yep, big mistake, he thought seconds later, after she'd pushed his shirt off his shoulders and her lips found that sensitive spot just below his ear. She worked his belt loose and lowered his zipper. Within seconds she'd swept off his clothes, her hands caressing every inch she exposed until he stood completely naked before his wife.

The spark of desire in her eyes nearly unraveled the last thin threads of his control. "Your turn to pay," he murmured.

Smiling, she ran her hands over his chest and around his neck. "That's what I was hoping for."

Hoarse laughter escaped him. "You're a nymph."

Her eyes grew as dark as navy, the candlelight flickering off the uncertainty that suddenly appeared in the velvet depths. "Are you complaining?" Her question was half teasing, half serious.

He brushed the back of his fingers across her cheek. "I

never did like silent, predictable lovemaking. You're anything but predictable, sweetheart.''

Reaching for the hem of her nightie, he shimmied the silky material up her thighs, across her belly and over her head, tossing the gown aside. Lowering his mouth to hers in a long, lingering kiss, he maneuvered her to the bed and guided her onto the soft mattress. He followed her down and pinned her there, the weight of his body settling between her spread thighs. Meshing their fingers at the side of her head, he stared into her eyes, an incredible feeling of want and need enveloping him.

Megan was awash with feeling, a swirl of thrilling sensations that made her breathless, dizzy and melting inside. She wanted to run her hands down his back, urge him to complete that downward move that would end the torment, but his hands kept hers locked. She wanted, oh, God, she wanted.... A whimper of frustration and need tangled in her throat.

His eyes glowed like hot emerald coals from the reflection of dying candlelight. ''You'll do anything for me?'' he asked in a low, rough voice, reminding her of the promise she'd made to him earlier.

She'd give him her heart and soul, if only he'd ask. But that wasn't what he was after. No, he wanted her total surrender. Through the passionate haze clouding her senses, she wondered how he intended to take it and experienced a shimmer of excitement that stripped all her inhibitions. *''Anything,''* she whispered.

''Wrap your legs around me. Tight.''

She did, and came undone when he consummated their marriage in a ritual as old as time and as sacred as the vows that made them husband and wife. He took her with a fierce kind of tenderness that touched her heart and brought her more pleasure than she thought she was capable of experiencing. When the tempest ebbed he kissed her so sweetly she wanted to weep. Her big, ferocious warrior with all his wounds and scars was the gentlest, most giving man she'd ever known.

But he'd never believe it.

Gently turning her, he tucked her body against his and wrapped his arms around her. "I think, Mrs. Fielding," he murmured sleepily into her ear, "that I could definitely get used to this."

I'm counting on it, Megan thought, her heart swelling with love and hope.

Megan woke alone, and although she wasn't totally surprised by Kane's absence, not waking with her new husband beside her still hurt. She'd hoped marriage would bring them closer, bridge some of the emotional distance that separated them. And for a few glorious hours last night she believed she'd reached past those barriers and touched a part of his soul.

Apparently, he was so used to withdrawing and shutting people out that he'd automatically done the same to her once the soft, warm glow of their lovemaking ebbed and cold reality intruded.

Sighing, she reached across the bed and placed her hand on his pillow. The gold band on her finger glinted, reminding her of the commitment she'd made to this man. She'd never taken her responsibilities lightly, and being Kane's wife would be no exception. She was going to love him whether he liked it or not, and she hoped that love would be enough to heal old pain and memories.

Mrs. Fielding. She smiled, liking her new name and the way it sounded on Kane's lips. She liked a lot about her husband, especially his smiles and laughter, rare gifts she intended to make a daily part of her life. Starting this morning.

Refusing to let Kane spend any of their short weekend honeymoon away from her or secluded in his workshop, she tossed off the covers and slid from the bed, intending to track her wayward husband. Passing the sexy nightie she'd worn the night before, she opted for comfort and grabbed one of his large shirts from the closet and slipped into it. She pulled on a pair of wispy panties then went into the bathroom and brushed her hair and teeth.

She returned to the bedroom and opened the top dresser drawer Kane had left empty for her undergarments. Reaching beneath the froth of silky things, she retrieved the wedding gift she'd bought for him when she'd gone into the city two days ago to do some shopping. Holding the silver-wrapped present against her chest, she padded down the hallway in search of Kane.

She found him in the kitchen, leaning against the open back door and staring at the yard. He wore a pair of soft faded jeans that made him look too sexy for her peace of mind. His pensive expression made her momentarily pause. They were good together in bed, but what about dealing with the everyday intimacies shared between a husband and wife? Would Kane allow them to have that kind of relationship or would he forever hide his emotions?

She wasn't going to let him. Determination propelled her forward, and he turned and looked at her. The instantaneous flare of hunger in his eyes caught her off guard, as did the spark of pure male possessiveness. Her body flushed from head to toe. The one thing he couldn't hide was his desire and physical response to her.

Gratified that she affected him on some level, she stopped at the kitchen table, waiting to see if he'd come to her. "Hi," she said, her voice sleep soft and a little husky from his open appraisal of her.

"Mornin'," he murmured, eyeing the present in her arms with a slight frown. He didn't move, increasing the awkward morning after tension filling the room.

They stood there for endless seconds, each one waiting for the other to make the first move. Finally, she gave in and crossed the distance separating them. Grabbing his hand, she led him to the table and pushed him into one of the wooden chairs, then draped herself over his lap before he could object.

The look of surprise on his face made her laugh. "I have something for you." She handed him the flat, square package, eager to see if he liked the gift she'd selected for him with such care.

Tentatively, he took the present. "My birthday isn't until November."

Sensing he wasn't used to receiving surprises, she sifted her fingers through the hair at his nape and smiled encouragingly. "I'll remember that for future reference. This, however, is a wedding gift."

His mouth tightened. "You didn't have to do that."

"I wanted to. I saw it when I went into the city and I knew you had to have it." Impatient and anxious to see his reaction, she nudged the gift in his hands. "Go ahead and open it."

"All right." He tore off the paper, revealing a thick, leather-bound book. He stilled, the wrappings fluttering to the floor unnoticed as he stared at the cover, the title and author inlaid in gold lettering.

"What's this for?" he asked, an odd, almost defensive quality to his voice.

She tilted her head curiously, certain he was teasing her. "It's for you. Open it up and take a look."

He did, slowly flipping through the pages. Glossy pictures of various pieces of furniture graced the pages, along with detailed instructions on how to build each. The pieces were intricate and elegant in design, requiring the skill of an experienced carpenter like Kane.

"I'm sure you have a collection of books on cabinetry," she said quickly when he said nothing, "but this is a new edition, and I couldn't resist." She searched his face, seeing a muscle in his cheek tick and something similar to anger darken his gaze.

Confusion doused her earlier exhilaration, and she touched his jaw, making him look at her. "You don't like it?" she asked, unable to keep the hurt from her voice.

Kane swallowed the huge knot in his throat and forcibly schooled his expression so he didn't disappoint her. He loved her thoughtfulness, but how could he like something that made him feel so inferior? Every time he looked at this leather-bound book he'd be reminded of the giant chasm that separated him and Megan. Other than the showy and striking pictures, he'd never be able to enjoy this book, never be able to duplicate one of the beautiful pieces of furniture for Megan like he suddenly wished he could, just to surprise her.

"It's great," he said, shoving his regret way down deep inside, to that dark place where it had lived for so many years. "But I have nothing to give you."

She gave a soft little sigh tinged with relief, which to his ears translated to, "*That's* why you looked so upset?" He'd let her think that because the truth might break the fragile bonds of his new marriage.

She shifted on his lap and rested her hands on his bare chest, her gaze capturing and holding his. "You've given me more than I ever possibly dreamed I would have."

"Andrew?" he guessed. He set the book on the table and dropped his hand to her knee, deciding he liked the way she looked in his shirt. Liking better, though, how she looked in nothing at all but a warm flush tingeing her body.

"Andrew, and you," she whispered.

"I'm not such a great bargain," he said gruffly, not wanting the responsibility of trying to remain balanced on that pedestal she was putting him on. One false move and he'd fall and break his neck.

"Oh, yes, you are." She smiled a siren's smile and wiggled her bottom. "I happen to think you're quite handy to have around."

Desire rocketed through him and he groaned, unable to resist her. "You're using me?" he teased.

"Absolutely. What's a husband for, if not to use properly?" She slowly unbuttoned the shirt she wore, revealing lush curves and smooth skin. And as Megan set out to seduce him and his body eagerly responded, a disturbing thought filtered through his mind.

His wife had discovered one of his weaknesses. Her.

Megan darted out of the bedroom from where she'd just changed into a short outfit and picked up the phone in the living room as it rang for the third time. She answered with a breathless hello.

Her greeting was met with silence, then a tentative female voice asked, "Is Kane there?"

She could still hear the water running in the bathroom where she'd left Kane ten minutes earlier, after they'd shared a morning shower. Megan found herself blushing at the memory, which was ridiculous. It wasn't as though the caller could read her thoughts.

"He's in the shower," she said, curious as to who this woman was and what she wanted Kane for. "Can I give him a message?"

Another pause. "This is his sister, Diane. Would Andrew happen to be there?"

"No, he's not." Realizing the intimate scene she'd just set for Kane's sister, she thought it wise to introduce herself before Diane jumped to the wrong conclusion. "I'm Megan, Kane's wife."

"Kane's wife?" Shock and disbelief filled Diane's exclamation. "Kane got married? Why didn't he tell me?"

"Everything happened so suddenly." And it had, a whirlwind of events that had irrevocably changed her and Kane's life. Knowing Diane would want details, she explained her friendship with Andrew and learned that Diane already knew of her from Andrew's letters. As for her marriage to Kane, she told her the same thing she'd told Mrs. Henderson, that she and Kane had been corresponding for the past year and a half and their long-distance relationship had evolved into something more. If Kane wanted to tell her the truth, she'd leave that to him.

She followed her brief story by saying, "I'm sure Kane was going to call to tell you the news."

"Hmph," Diane said indignantly. "Kane is terrible about calling, and he's even worse about answering my letters—which he's never, ever done. But maybe that's because he's been spending all his time writing to you." Her voice held a teasing quality.

Megan didn't correct her assumption, but she did find it odd that Kane wouldn't respond to his sister's letters.

"I'm sure I would have found out sooner or later from Andrew that my big brother got married," Diane went on. "At least *he* writes me faithfully."

Megan smiled. "I'll make sure he continues to do so."

"Good," Diane said, sounding satisfied. Then she grew more heartfelt. "Megan, take care of my brother for me, okay? He's been through so much. He raised me after our parents died, and I know he didn't have an easy marriage with Cathy. It was so difficult for me to move away and leave him, but my husband got a better paying job, and, well, we have a young family of our own and knew he'd never be able to make the kind of money he is now if we stayed in Linden. But I miss Kane and Andrew so much."

Megan was certain the sentiment was returned by both Andrew and Kane. "I'll have to see what I can do about coercing Kane into taking us on a vacation."

"Oh, please do!" Diane said excitedly.

They talked for a few minutes longer. By the time Kane exited the bedroom and she handed him the phone so his sister could congratulate him on his new marriage, Megan felt as though she and Diane had forged the beginning of a friendship.

And as Megan sauntered into the kitchen to give Kane some privacy, she decided she liked having a real family of her own, complete with the sister she'd never had but always wanted.

CHAPTER EIGHT

KANE arrived home from work the following Thursday afternoon expecting Joyce's car to be parked out front as it normally was. It wasn't. He was surprised she'd left without her weekly pay, which he gave to her after he cashed his check on Thursdays. Maybe Megan had paid Joyce after her tutoring session with Andy, he thought, climbing out of his truck.

Megan. They'd been married less than a week, but already they'd settled into a comfortable pattern shared by married couples. He looked forward to coming home and seeing her, sitting at the kitchen table, eating dinner and talking about everyone's day. Just like a real family. Andy had asked Megan if he could call her mom, and the delight and love shining in her eyes had warmed Kane. Despite his personal reservations about marrying Megan, he knew he'd done the right thing for his son.

He entered the kitchen, set his lunch box on the counter, then followed the voices drifting from the living room. Megan and Andy sat on the couch together with Andy reading from a textbook while Megan followed along and helped him pronounce the more complicated words.

"Where's Joyce?"

Megan glanced up, startled.

Andy stopped reading and put a bookmark between the pages before closing it. "Hi, Dad. Joyce isn't here."

"She didn't show up for your lesson?" It wasn't like Joyce to be so irresponsible.

"She was right on time," Megan said, straightening the school papers scattered on the coffee table. "I paid her for the week and sent her home."

He stopped in the middle of the room, frowning. "Is she sick?"

"No." Finally, Megan looked up, meeting his gaze. A hint of defiance shimmered in the depths. "I let her go."

"You *what?*" His voice rose an octave.

Megan didn't flinch. "I said I let her go."

"As in she won't be back?"

"Yes."

He gaped at her, unable to believe she'd be so bold. He could feel his world shifting, throwing him off balance. He struggled to find even ground. "You let her go without asking me?"

"I thought we'd discuss it tonight," she replied reasonably.

He wasn't feeling reasonable. "I'd like to discuss it *now.*" He turned and strode into the kitchen.

He heard his son's plea. "Mom, please make him understand."

He heard Megan's soft response. "I'll try my best."

He paced the floor, a jumbled mass of emotions twisting inside him. Needing a release, he vented his anger on Megan as soon as she entered the room.

"You had no right to get rid of Joyce." He jammed his hands on his hips and pinned her with an incensed look. He knew he was acting irrational but he couldn't help himself. "I hired a tutor for Andy for a reason!"

She crossed her arms over her chest, not backing down at his ferocious glare. "Which is?"

Kane froze. Too late, he realized his mistake. Only one reason managed to filter through his muddled mind. *I want him to have all the advantages I never had as a kid. I want him to be able to go to college and be successful one day.* But he couldn't voice his explanation because his reasons intertwined with his insecurities and childhood memories of forgetting school lessons. Of wanting to learn but being so overwhelmed by other responsibilities that he'd had to forfeit an education.

And now, as an adult, he paid for that sacrifice every day of his life. He'd vowed long ago that Andrew would never know the degradation and humiliation of not being academically inclined.

Of not knowing how to read.

But Megan seemed to understand even without knowing the truth. Her expression softened, and she approached him. "I know you want the best for Andrew, but I talked to Mrs. Graham today and found out he's well above most of his classmates."

"A tutor keeps him there," he replied tightly.

"Andrew is a smart kid. He told me only the kids with learning disabilities have tutors."

He released a harsh breath that whistled between his teeth. Turning away, he pushed his fingers through his hair, wondering if he'd inadvertently damaged his son's self-confidence. He'd never intended to make Andy feel inferior, had only meant to give him every benefit possible. It pained him that he'd hurt his son that way, yet a part of him didn't regret his decision.

"Dad?"

Kane looked at Andrew, who stood in the kitchen doorway, an uncertain expression on his face. "Yes?"

He fidgeted on his sneakered feet. "I don't want Joyce to tutor me anymore."

Kane couldn't quite let go of his convictions. "Son, sometimes we have to do things we don't like—"

Megan placed a firm hand on Kane's arm, halting his lecture. "Kane, you need to listen to Andrew."

He clenched his jaw, but he looked at his son.

"I like Joyce," Andrew went on, "but it's not like she teaches me things I don't already know."

"She helps you with your homework," Kane pointed out. And that was something he *couldn't* do.

Andrew's gaze went from Kane to Megan. The two exchanged a look before he glanced at his dad again. "Mom can help me with my homework."

Kane rubbed the taut muscles at the back of his neck, debating the merits of such an arrangement.

Megan's fingers tightened around the corded muscles in

his forearm. "Since I'm here when he gets home from school, I'll be able to spend time reviewing his homework with him."

"Please, Dad," Andrew begged. "I don't need Joyce. I got straight As on my last report card."

"What if your grades start slipping?"

"If that happens, which I doubt," Megan said wryly, letting Kane know with a pointed look that she wouldn't allow it to happen, "then we'll rehire Joyce."

Kane could feel his arguments crumbling. He couldn't protect Andrew forever, and he knew he needed to extend his son some trust or Andrew would grow to resent him and the tutoring. The only thing that eased his mind was that Megan would be able to monitor his progress.

"Deal?" Andrew asked enthusiastically, thrusting a hand toward Kane before he could formulate any more questions or change his mind.

Kane knew when he was beaten and accepted defeat gracefully. "Deal," he muttered, and shook the hand Andrew offered.

"Andy, get dressed for church," Kane called as he followed the delicious aroma of coffee down the hallway. "We're leaving in half an hour."

"Okay, Dad!" Andy darted around him to the bathroom, Sunday clothes in hand.

Kane entered the kitchen. Megan glanced from the tablet of paper in front of her, pen poised for jotting down items in a neat row.

"Good morning," Kane greeted her cheerfully. He opened the refrigerator and peered at the meager contents.

She tapped the end of her pen against her paper, lifting a brow. "You're in an awfully good mood this morning."

He looked over his shoulder, smiling lazily. "Is there any reason not to be?"

"I suppose not." Amusement and soft desire sparkled in her blue eyes. "All you have time for is a quick bowl of cereal."

"I'll pass." He closed the refrigerator door and approached the table. "We'll grab some lunch after church."

She laced her fingers beneath her chin and gave him a chastising look. "I would have made you a big breakfast if you hadn't kept pressing the snooze button."

He flicked the tail end of her braid over her shoulder, letting his fingers linger on the satiny skin of her neck. "Handy little thing to have on an alarm clock, isn't it?"

"We didn't sleep." The shiver rippling down the length of her spine contradicted her prim tone.

He propped his hip against the edge of the table in front of her. His calf pressed into her thigh, and her gaze flew to his. "I don't remember hearing you complain, sweetheart," he said in a low, husky voice. Lightly pressing his thumb to her bottom lip, he dragged it across the full swell. "But then again, that mouth of yours was busy doin' other things."

Her breath quickened, and she pulled back out of his reach. "Kane, stop."

She didn't want him to stop, not really. He recognized the want in her gaze and the flush spreading from the neckline of her pretty pink floral dress. But they had Andrew to consider, and that was the *only* reason he kept his hands to himself.

So, instead, he leaned forward and pressed a quick kiss to her parted lips, murmuring, "I like it when you blush." Straightening, he grabbed her empty coffee mug. "Want a refill?"

Waking from her sensual fog, she glanced at the delicate gold watch on her wrist, noting the time. "Please. With cream and a spoonful of sugar."

He went to the coffeemaker, and she picked up her pen and jotted a few more items on her growing list. He filled both mugs and added a splash of cream to hers. He opened the cupboard and searched the contents for the pink and white bag of sugar he kept on the second shelf.

It was gone, and it had been a full two-pound bag.

Assuming Megan must have used it for her baking, he said, "Add sugar to your grocery list. We're out."

"Oh, I forgot to tell you, I put the sugar, salt, flour and coffee in the canisters."

Frowning, he closed the cupboard door and turned. "What canisters?" His tone sounded as cautious as he felt, like he'd been suddenly thrust into a mine field and had to watch every step or be blown to smithereens.

She continued scribbling on her notepad. "The ones on the counter."

His gaze scanned the counter, spotting not one, but four ceramic containers with a flower design and bold letters on the front of each. His body tensed. They hadn't been there yesterday morning.

"Where did the canisters come from?" He forced a neutral tone.

"They're mine. I unpacked them from the stuff Judi sent. I thought they perked up the kitchen. Do you like them?"

"Yeah, they're great," he muttered.

He hated them. He hated change of any kind even more. He liked the kitchen the way it was, had arranged the cupboards so he knew where everything was located and could find it blindfolded if he needed to. But he couldn't tell her that without her getting upset or suspicious.

"Which one's the sugar?" he asked casually.

"It's right on the label." She stopped her writing long enough to give him a peculiar look over her shoulder. "I'm sure you can figure it out for yourself."

Sure he could. He always did. He knew from experience there would be plenty of these situations, but it had been over five years since he'd had to scramble for excuses and responses. If he wasn't careful, the truth wouldn't remain a secret for long.

Carrying her coffee, he approached the canisters, eyeing them warily. The letters emblazoned across them mocked him. The land mine beneath his feet rumbled with every step. He was determined to get through this without letting the situation blow up in his face.

Get used to bluffing, Kane. You've got a hell of a lot of years ahead of you. Besides, deception has been a part of your life for so long it should be second nature. So why was Megan different? Why did she make him feel like a fumbling kid trying to stay two steps ahead of the game?

He opened the lid on the first canister and found white granules. Bingo. He rounded off a teaspoon and hesitated, remembering that she'd mentioned salt, too. Giving Megan a surreptitious glance to be certain she was otherwise occupied, he licked his pinky finger, brushed it over the granules and tasted it. And winced. Salt. Wouldn't that have been an eye opener for Megan, in more ways than one?

The second canister held dark brown coffee grounds, and the contents of the third container looked like the same substance as was in the first. Not taking any chances, he sampled the sweet granules, then dumped a spoonful into Megan's coffee.

Megan glanced at Kane as he placed the steaming mug in front of her. She took a sip, savoring the creamy taste. "Mm, it's perfect. Thank you."

He slid into the chair next to her. "Anytime."

"I'll be going grocery shopping tomorrow after Andy goes to school. Can you think of anything other than what's on my list that you might want or need?" She pushed her list in front of him for his review. "It's going to take me a few tries to figure out what you and Andrew like and dislike, but I'd appreciate your input."

He picked up the tablet and looked at the list. After a few moments he handed it back without comment. "We like just about everything except lima beans and liver."

"You're easy to please. Any favorites?"

He grinned, looking like a young boy. "Twinkies and home-made spaghetti."

"That's quite a combination." She added a few items to her list. "So, do you want to add anything to the list?"

"Nope. Buy whatever you need." Withdrawing his wallet from his pants pocket, he counted off some twenty-dollar bills and tossed them her way. "Will that cover it?"

"Uh, sure," she said, feeling funny about taking his cash so freely, despite them being husband and wife. "If not, I have some extra money on me."

"I'll pay for anything you might need."

Kane's pride was showing, she thought, understanding his insistence. Especially since she knew the money problems he'd had in his marriage to Cathy and his need to support his family. But couldn't two contribute to the burden?

Wrapping her hands around her mug, she leaned back in her chair and took a sip of coffee. "There's something I've been wanting to ask you."

"What's that?"

She shifted in her seat, suddenly feeling awkward and unsure. They hadn't had a normal courtship, time to talk about the little matters involved in a marriage and how they'd settle them or the different compromises they'd make. In so many ways they knew so little about one another, but they needed to learn to communicate openly. And she'd always believed financial obligations should be a shared venture.

She asked her question before she lost the nerve. "How do you feel about opening a joint checking account?"

"Not interested." His tone was firm and final.

"I'll contribute my share of funds," she automatically said, wanting him to know theirs was an equal partnership, the royalties she made on her books included in on the deal. "And you can still keep your own personal checking account if you'd like—"

"I don't have a checking account, nor do I want one. My savings account is all I need."

She gaped at him. A checking account was essential to everyday life. She couldn't imagine not having one. "You're serious?"

He stared at her steadily, silently answering her question.

"Then how do you pay for things?"

The corner of his mouth quirked, but the dark shadows

clouding his gaze overrode the glimpse of dry humor. "Cash seems to work just fine."

She shook her head incredulously. "You pay all your bills with cash?"

A muscle in his cheek twitched. "Yes. You have a problem with that?"

She frowned at his sharp, defensive tone. "It's just that you'd save so much time if you just wrote a check and dropped the bill into the mail instead of running all over town settling up with everyone."

Slowly, he stood, towering over her. He held her gaze with challenge and the simmering heat of anger. Very quietly, he said, "If you don't like my method, then *you* pay the bills."

Two days later Megan pulled into the parking lot of the town's only bank, the Linden Trust and Loan, still pondering Kane's angry reaction to her suggestion of a joint checking account. She had no intention of taking over his finances, and had told him as much. Her reassurance had been met with a scowl before Andrew had interrupted the heated moment.

Sighing heavily, she parked the car in an empty stall and turned off the ignition. Her husband's erratic behavior bewildered and intrigued her. Tender and teasing one moment, cool and distant the next, all because of a stupid checking account.

It wasn't as though she planned to spend his money frivolously, she thought, exiting the car and starting toward the red brick building. She was a saver by nature and thought a joint checking account might simplify their finances.

Yet he'd never had a checking account and only dealt with cash, which she thought as odd in today's high-tech world of bank machines and credit-card checking. But when she'd questioned him on his uncommon practice, he'd been defensive and unwilling to compromise, acting as though her suggestion threatened his entire way of life. Not wanting to allow something that trivial to drive a wedge between them, she'd let it drop.

When they'd arrived home from church that afternoon, alone since Andrew was at the Lindens, he'd pulled her into his arms and had kissed her with a passionate urgency that melted the tension between them. He was a proud man, and she supposed that had been his way of silently apologizing, which she'd accepted with her own acquiescence.

He was good at that, she mused, making her forget everything but what he did to her. Although she admitted it was a pleasant way to make up, nothing was resolved afterward.

Shaking off her thoughts, she entered the bank. The financial institution was small, with three teller windows—two currently in use—a section for loans and new accounts and a sitting area for customers. The place was decorated in warm rust tones with greenery for accents.

She headed toward the pretty brunette sitting behind the new accounts desk. A gold name tag on her dress proclaimed her Debbie Davis, Accounts Manager.

The young woman smiled congenially. "Welcome to Linden Trust and Loan," she recited. "How may I help you?"

Before Megan could respond, the phone on the desk buzzed and a female voice said, "Debbie, Ms. Peterson is on line one about her trust account."

Debbie gave Megan an apologetic look. "If you'll excuse me, I'll be just a minute," she said, picking up the line.

Megan nodded her understanding and stepped away from the desk to give the accounts manager some privacy with her customer. Her gaze glanced by the only two offices in the bank and skittered back. She read the gold nameplates beside the doors. Jack Hamilton, Vice President. His office light was off. Moving on to the next office, she smiled. Harold Linden, President. His light was on.

While Debbie argued with the woman on the phone about the eligibility requirements of her trust account,

Megan strolled a few feet away until she could verify that Harold was in his office. He was. She caught a profile of him as he leaned back in a leather executive chair, a pair of glasses perched on his nose as he read a document in his hand. She moved toward Debbie's desk, an idea taking shape.

The woman hung up the phone and clasped her hands on the desk, giving Megan her undivided attention. "Now, where were we?"

"You were asking how you could help me." Megan kept her face expressionless. "I'm here to see Mr. Linden."

Debbie looked momentarily confused. "Do you have an appointment?"

"No, but I'm sure he'll see me." Megan wished she felt as confident as she sounded. What if he refused to see her? Worse, what if he ordered her out of the bank? No, she'd expect that kind of behavior from Patricia, but Harold seemed more reasonable.

The young woman frowned, the first stirring of skepticism entering her gaze. "And you are?"

"Megan. Megan Fielding."

Debbie's hazel eyes widened. "Oh," she breathed, as if to say, *So, you're the one everyone's been talking about.* "I, uh, I'm not sure if he's in right now."

Megan understood the employee's protectiveness toward her boss, but she only wanted to talk to Harold without the ominous presence of his wife to influence him. *If* he would see her. She could barge into his office, but she didn't want to make a scene. Besides, that wasn't her style. Whatever the rift between the Lindens and Kane, she wanted to try to settle it civilly.

It didn't matter that Kane would be furious with her for interfering.

Megan smiled patiently and adjusted the strap of her purse on her shoulder. "Unless that's his twin I saw sitting at his desk, I'd say he's in."

Debbie looked decidedly frazzled. She picked up the

phone and pressed three digits. "Mr. Linden, I'm sorry to disturb you, but there's a Megan Fielding here to see you."

Megan heard the echo of Harold's voice drifting from his office but couldn't decipher what he'd said. She found out as soon as Debbie hung up the receiver.

The accounts manager pointed beyond Megan. "He said he'll see you. His office is that way."

Harold met her at the door to his office, subdued interest playing over his features. He wore a stylish gray pin-striped suit and a paisley print tie. Despite his age and thinning gray hair, Megan thought he was a very handsome man.

"Mrs. Fielding," he acknowledged politely, looking as though the name brought memories that pained him.

"Megan, please," she said, wanting to dispense with formalities.

He smiled gratefully, and she could see kindness in his eyes. "Megan, what can I do for you?"

"I'd like to open a checking account."

He lifted a gray brow. "Debbie would be happy to help you."

Megan wasn't about to be deterred. All she needed was a few moments alone with Harold, to see if there was any chance of a reconciliation between him and his wife and Kane. "I have a substantial amount of money to transfer, and I'd feel more secure dealing with you." She nearly cringed at her pathetic excuse.

A faint smile tipped the corner of his mouth. "I know having the title of president sounds impressive, but in reality I depend on my employees to run my bank smoothly and efficiently. I could fumble my way through all the paperwork for your new checking account and transfers, but the fact is, Debbie is far more adept at the procedure than I am."

Megan blew out an exasperated breath. "All right, I'll save the accounts for Debbie, but I'd like to talk to you about Kane and Andrew."

He didn't seem surprised, and more important, he didn't turn her away. "Why don't you come in and have a seat?"

"Thank you." She entered his office, and he closed the door on the gawking patrons and employees.

Sitting in one of the wing chairs in front of his desk, she inhaled the scent of leather and pipe tobacco. Harold settled into his chair behind his mahogany desk, the smooth surface cluttered with files and reports. Now that she was here, she didn't know what to say.

Harold broke the ice. "Belated congratulations on your marriage to Kane."

His genuine sentiment surprised her. "Doesn't my marrying Kane bother you?"

He leaned back in his chair, a thoughtful expression on his face. "I'll admit I was shocked by the news, as most of us were, but Andrew thinks very highly of you, and he's happier than I've ever seen him. His welfare is my first concern."

Megan settled her purse beside her on the chair, feeling more at ease with Harold than she thought she would. And comfortable enough to pursue her goal. "Is that how Patricia feels?"

He frowned, making the wrinkles on his forehead more prominent. "Of course she does."

"Then why does she insist on playing tug-of-war with Andrew's emotions?"

"We do no such thing," he replied indignantly. "We love Andrew very much and would never hurt him that way."

"But you are, intentionally or not." She sat forward, not wanting to insult him but needing him to understand why an affable agreement between families was so important. "By alienating yourselves from Kane you're putting Andrew right in the middle of your feud. The tension between the three of you is awful, and although Andrew may accept your behavior because he's so young, he doesn't know any better, and he may come to resent all three of you later for making him choose between you and his father."

Regret filled Harold's brown eyes. "I know," he said softly.

Confusion rippled through Megan. "Then why do you allow this dissension to continue when it can all end with a few simple words?"

Harold stood, a weary sadness passing over his features. For a fleeting moment Megan thought he was going to ask her to leave, but he walked to the floor-to-ceiling window that overlooked the slow pace of Linden. He faced her and said, "Because my wife has never forgiven Kane for what he did to our daughter."

Unable to believe the Lindens could be so shallow as to hold Kane responsible for what happened to Cathy, Megan's stomach sank like a lead weight. She joined Harold at the window, ready to defend her husband. "What Kane did was own up to his responsibilities and marry the woman he got pregnant."

He looked at her, obviously surprised by her knowledge of Kane's relationship with Cathy. "He told you?"

"Yes," she said quietly. "He also told me he loved Cathy very much."

"And you must love Kane to go to this extreme."

She smiled, unable to hide her feelings for her new family. "I love Kane and Andrew very much, and I don't want either of them to be hurt by something that can be easily fixed."

He sighed, suddenly looking much older than she believed him to be. "Megan, I know Kane isn't a bad person—"

"Than how can you let everyone believe he killed your daughter?"

He cringed and flushed in embarrassment. "No one really *believes* he killed her."

She stared at him in disbelief. "That's even worse. He feels responsible for her emotional state when she died. The rumors about him killing her only compound his guilt."

"I never knew."

How could he have known when Kane wouldn't let anyone close enough to learn the truth? The only reason she'd been privy to such information was that she'd practically pried it from him. "If a person hears something about themselves enough times they tend to believe it. How can you let a horrible lie like that keep circulating?"

"I didn't, not intentionally." Shaking his head, he moved away from the window to the credenza behind his desk. "As shameful as this might sound, I think it was easier for Patricia to cope with Cathy's death if she could blame Kane rather than believe the truth."

Megan crossed her arms over her chest and remained where she stood, not wanting to shatter this fragile moment of revelations. "Which is?"

Picking up a brass-framed photograph, he gazed at the picture of his young, beautiful daughter. When he finally looked at Megan, grief and loss shone in his eyes. "That we spoiled Cathy, and she married Kane with too many expectations."

Megan had learned as much talking to Kane, but hearing Harold confirm it gave her an unexpected rush of relief. "Kane did the best he could to support his family."

"I know that, but I never could refuse Cathy anything. She was our only child and knew just how to wrap me around her finger." Harold rubbed his thumb over the glossy photo, a sad smile on his face. "When she asked me to give Kane a job here at the bank, I thought of it as a good employment opportunity for Kane and a way of keeping the business in the family. But most men do have their pride."

"Kane has plenty of that," Megan murmured wryly.

Harold set the frame on the credenza and lowered himself into his chair. "His father, Tom, was the same way. Very stubborn, but a hard worker. I respect that about Kane, but I also hoped he'd accept the job so he could take over the reins of the banking business after I retired."

"I don't think Kane was cut out to wear a suit and tie," she said lightly, remembering what Kane told her the night they'd discussed this topic.

"I think I always knew that." He steepled his fingers in front of him, his expression thoughtful. "Kane had such a hard life. He lost his parents at an early age and raised his sister on his own. He never seemed to want anything beyond the ordinary and was quite satisfied working at the sawmill. Cathy wanted to mold Kane into something he wasn't. I know their marriage was strained after he refused my job offer, and Cathy...well, she was unhappy because she wanted more than what Kane was capable of giving her."

Megan dragged a hand through her hair, seeing the situation from two very different perspectives. She crossed to her chair and sat down.

"Patricia and I argued about Cathy's situation," he went on. "She thought Cathy should leave Kane, and I told her we needed to stay out of their business and let them work out their problems on their own. I thought it was a good dose of reality for Cathy, who'd had everything handed to her her entire life. She had a family of her own and needed to learn that sometimes there were sacrifices to make in a marriage. But Cathy was young and spoiled and made sure that everyone knew how miserable she was once Kane made it clear he wouldn't take the job I offered." He drew a long, shuddering breath. "And when she died, Patricia fell apart. The easiest thing for her to do was blame Kane."

There was so much hurt on both sides, Megan realized. She ached for the Lindens' loss, but they couldn't continue blaming Kane for something he had no control over. Forgetting the past was impossible, but together they had to work on forgiving and building a new future. "This rift has got to stop."

Harold discreetly wiped away a bit of moisture gathering on his bottom lashes. "It's gone on for so long, I don't think any of us know how to end it."

But he wanted to. She could see it in his eyes. And that was a start. "You have to, for Andrew." She wasn't above using his grandson for leverage, not if that's what it took to bring these two broken families together.

Harold nodded in understanding. "What can I do?"

"Well, for starters, we need to get Patricia and Kane together, to make them realize what we already know. Unfortunately, Kane is too proud to come forward on his own."

"And Patty is too stubborn."

"Then it'll have to be up to us." She leaned toward him, renewed enthusiasm lacing her voice. "How about if you bring her over for dinner, let's say two weeks from this Friday? That should be enough time to convince her to talk to Kane."

A crooked smile creased his mouth. "I think I'd have more luck bringing her over without any warning."

He had a point, she thought, considering how much these two would resist a reconciliation. "Yes, that might be the best thing for Kane, too, no time to contemplate or get angry."

"Megan," Harold said hesitantly, "don't expect too much. So many years have passed that it might take some time to get Patricia to accept Kane and you as part of the family."

Picking up her purse, she stood. "I know, but it's worth a try, for Andrew's benefit." Beneath all Patricia's heartache and resentment there had to be enough compassion to give Andrew the family he deserved.

He smiled warmly. "Yes, you're right. We'll give it our best shot." He came around the big desk that separated them, hand extended, his gaze expressing his gratitude. She slipped her slender fingers into his. "Thank you for stopping by. Andrew is very lucky to have you as a stepmother."

"I'm even luckier to have him. He's a wonderful little boy, and I only want the best for him." She withdrew her hand and started for the door. "I'll be in touch, Harold."

"I hope you enjoyed the champagne."

One hand on the doorknob, Megan stilled. She glanced over her shoulder, tilting her head curiously. Had he been the friend who sent them their bottle of champagne? "Pardon?"

If she hadn't been looking so closely, she would have missed his quick wink and the twinkle in his eyes. "I said, have a good day."

She grinned. "Thank you, we did..." *Enjoy the champagne,* she thought. "I mean, I will. Have a good day, that is."

CHAPTER NINE

KANE sat on the living room couch, the light from the lamp reflecting off the glossy color pages of the hardbound book Megan had given him as a wedding gift.

He couldn't sleep, despite it being past two in the morning. His body was satiated from making love with Megan, but emotionally, he experienced a restlessness he couldn't shake. And while prowling around the house, he'd been inexplicably drawn to the woodworking book he'd avoided since the day he'd been given the gift. Alone, without someone watching his every reaction, without fearing some question that would be related to the text in the book, he was free to absorb and analyze the illustrations. He was determined to create one of the designs without a pattern, just to prove to himself that he could. Another challenge in a lifetime of frustrating obstacles.

After a while the pictures in front of him blurred as his mind drifted to the woman he'd left in his bed. A woman who was getting under his skin and making him feel things he didn't want to feel. A woman who had the ability to infuriate him and provoke him. With just a simple look or touch she chased away the loneliness that had been his constant companion for so long. How could that be when he'd vowed never to open himself to another woman that way?

Nearly a week had passed since the joint checking account debacle. He'd been a jerk about the situation, but fortunately for him, Megan was easy to distract with kisses and caresses, and she was quick to forgive. He liked that about her. He liked her smiles and teasing and his name on her lips when he slid deep inside her. He only wished he could be more for her.

What he didn't like were the changes she was making to

his home, no matter how subtle the transformations. Finding his clothes in different drawers and discovering bathroom supplies reorganized was enough to give him an anxiety attack. So far, the worst that had happened was she'd cleaned out his medicine cabinet in the bathroom, rearranged his toiletries on one shelf and added her feminine products, most of which he didn't recognize by box or container.

The variety of stuff she used had overwhelmed him. His needs in that department were simple—shaving cream, deodorant and toothpaste. He found himself snooping when he was alone, opening bottles that looked like perfume and sniffing the contents, spraying cans of stuff that smelled like hair spray and deodorant, testing jars and tubes of creams for future reference.

As if his thoughts had conjured her, she padded toward him, sleep-tousled and wearing the shirt he'd worn that evening. Their eyes met, and something passed between them. Not a sexual charge, but something infinitely more intimate. An emotion so intense and deep it tugged on his soul. And scared the hell out of him, because whatever the emotion was, he wanted to experience it with her.

Closing the book, he straightened. "What are you doing up?"

She smiled sleepily. "I could ask you the same thing, but I think the answer is obvious."

"It is?" Could she detect his innermost thoughts, feelings and fears?

"Neither of us can sleep," she said, stating the obvious. Sinking onto the cushion beside him, she curled her bare legs beneath her and snuggled up to his side. "I'm glad to see you like your book. I wasn't sure if you did or not."

He gently brushed unruly strands of hair from her cheek. "Didn't I thank you properly?"

"Yes, very thoroughly, but you just seemed so..." She shrugged, as if the right word eluded her.

He didn't want her to finish that, knowing he'd made love to her that morning as much to distract her as to forget the confusing, conflicting emotions raging inside him. "It's the nicest gift I've ever received." That much was the truth. No one had ever given him something with so much thought and care behind the gesture.

She smiled radiantly. "I'm glad, because you deserve it."

He set the book on the coffee table, wanting to tell her he didn't deserve something he couldn't fully enjoy, and he didn't deserve her caring and kindness. Coward that he was, the words remained anchored.

She moved closer until her legs pressed against his jeans-clad thigh and her head rested on his bare chest, her warm breath fanning his skin. Closing his eyes, he drew in her scent, cherishing the feel of her. A shiver passed through her, and she cuddled more fully into him.

"Cold?" he asked.

"Umm."

"Would you like to go back to bed, or would you like me to make a fire?"

She tipped her head, giving him a sultry, upswept glance. "That's a difficult choice, but considering we can always go to bed *after* a fire, having one would be nice."

"Who says we have to go back to bed at all when we have a perfectly good couch out here?" he said, leaving her to build a fire.

"Did you make this china hutch?"

Kane glanced over his shoulder to the far side of the room where Megan stood. He hadn't heard her get up from the couch, and he had no idea why she'd care if he'd made that hutch, unless... "Does it look handmade?"

"Not especially." She examined the top piece, made of pine and beveled glass doors, then bent, tracing her fingers along the scrolled grooves he'd carved into the bottom casing. "It's beautifully crafted, not something that looks like it's been manufactured in an assembly line at some furniture factory."

Her compliment stroked his ego just enough to make him

admit the truth. "I made that for mine and Cathy's first wedding anniversary."

She straightened, her gaze curious. "How come it's empty?"

He dropped another log on the licking flames. "Cathy wanted a matching dinette set, which I never got around to making." *I don't want mismatched furniture that doesn't have a brand name, Kane. It makes it look like we buy our furniture from garage sales.* After Cathy's comment, he'd lost the inspiration to complete the set.

"This piece is beautiful all by itself."

Only an extraordinary woman like Megan would think so, he thought, prodding a burning log with the steel poker. He wondered if she'd be so impressed with his talent if he told her he was illiterate, that he was self-taught and most likely put things together backward and somehow managed to get it right.

"I have some china and crystal that I haven't unpacked yet. Would you mind if I put them in here?"

He shrugged and placed the poker on its hook, then adjusted the screen. "If you really want to."

"Of course I want to." She crossed the room and sat on her knees next to him. "Quit being so modest, Kane."

He settled his back against the couch, thinking modesty had nothing to do with it. "I'm sure you'd prefer something better and fancier."

She crawled over to him, looking like a sleek cat. The firelight spun gold into her hair and made her eyes sparkle like sapphires. "The hutch is perfect. Elegant and understated," she said, kneeling between his legs, her face inches from his. "I don't like fancy."

Her sass made him grin. The hands she placed on his thighs caused his body to respond accordingly. He held his desire in check. "All women like nice things."

"Hmm. Depends on your definition of nice." Her eyes drifted closed, and she skimmed her hands over his hips and his belly, blazing her own brand of fire all the way up his chest and around his neck. "This," she whispered, her lips nuzzling his, "is *nice*."

Groaning, he tumbled her across his lap and into his arms. He plunged his fingers into her hair, his pulse picking up its beat, matching the rhythm of hers. "Yeah, this is *real* nice."

He kissed her, long and slow, in no hurry to end the lazy, playful intimacy they shared. Finally, he lifted his mouth, satisfied with the dreamy quality of Megan's expression.

She sighed contentedly and settled herself so her bottom nestled into the crux of his thighs. He wrapped his arms around her waist, propped his chin on her shoulder and stared at the bright, crackling fire.

She slid her hands over his and twined their fingers together over her belly. "Have you ever thought about selling your work?"

Too many times to count, but selling required paperwork, which isn't something I have a knack for. "Who would buy it?"

"I would."

Her unconditional confidence in him made him *almost* believe in himself. Closing his eyes, he buried his face in the softness of her neck, absorbing her warmth and gentleness in its purest sense. "You're my wife. You're supposed to feel that way."

She turned in his arms until she could look at him. "I'm not biased." She feigned an indignant look, the laughter dancing in her gaze a dead giveaway. Then she grew serious. "I'd bet, if you tried, you could find a place in the city where you could sell your furniture and toys on consignment."

He gave his head a firm shake. Consignment equaled paperwork and filling out invoices. "I don't think so."

"Why not?" she persisted. "You have the ability to make a living doing what you love. Your workmanship is proof that you have an incredible talent and knack for creating beautiful things."

The trust and certainty in her expression twisted Kane's stomach into a knot. She was so completely open and honest with him, and he'd never given her anything but a tangled mess of lies and deceit, even if they were unspoken ones. Deception and bluffing had never bothered him much before, so why was he having an attack of conscience now? Because she put so much faith in him, and he didn't deserve even a sliver of it. When it came down to stripping off the facade, he didn't have the guts to do it and risk the painful repercussions.

Reflexively, he tightened his arms around her. "It's just a hobby, Megan. Nothing more."

"You know, writing was once my hobby."

He welcomed the change in subject. "You didn't always write?"

"Well, yes...kind of."

"Kind of?"

"I didn't start out as a professional writer, but I always wrote in a journal, if that counts for anything. I'm a legal secretary by trade. I started writing after my divorce. Being a published writer was always a distant dream, but I wanted to be a children's writer so badly that I made the dream come true. It took a lot of hard work and rejections from many publishers, but I finally got an offer and a series of my own. And I couldn't be happier with my choice." She smiled softly, encouragingly. "I believe in you, Kane. But you have to believe in yourself before you can believe in your work."

"You make it sound so easy." He *wanted* it to be that easy.

"It is. I believe in your talent and ability."

He wished that was enough. "Yeah, well, I'm not one to take chances." The odds were against him.

She lifted her fingers to the stubble covering his jaw, her touch light and reverent. "You took a chance with me."

His throat jammed with a hundred different emotions he couldn't define. Stealing an opportunity to end their conversation and make him forget, for a little while, what he'd never have, he slid a hand down her back and maneuvered her gently to the floor, easing his body over the length of hers.

"You, if I recall correctly, Mrs. Fielding," he murmured, dipping his head to plant teasing kisses on her lips, "were a sure thing."

"Kane, could I see you in my office, please?"

Jeff's request put Kane instantly on guard, especially since Jeff had never summoned him to his office in the year and a half he'd been in charge of the mill. He wondered what was wrong.

Kane picked up a freshly cut board and placed it on the pile behind him. "Be right there, boss."

Five minutes later Kane walked into Jeff's office. He removed his leather gloves, tucked them into the back pocket of his jeans and approached the steel desk where his boss sat.

Jeff looked up from a file spread open in front of him. "Have a seat, Kane."

Lowering himself to one of the Naugahyde chairs, he tried to relax his suddenly tense body. "Is there a problem?" he asked gruffly.

"Yes, there is." Jeff ruffled through the papers in the file and pulled one out. "I know I've only been in charge of the mill the last couple of years since my father died, and it's taken me a while to get up to speed on everyone. I've been reviewing your employee file and I've noticed you've topped your wages in your position."

Kane's jaw tightened. "I'm satisfied with my wages."

Jeff eyed him steadily, making Kane uncomfortable. "You've passed up numerous promotions."

"I'm satisfied where I'm at."

An odd look passed over Jeff's features. Then he went on, either not having heard how satisfied Kane was or purposely dismissing his claim. "Roy Peters just gave me two weeks notice. He's moving to California. There's a position open in purchasing, and I'd like to offer it to you."

"No." Kane's answer was quick and instinctive.

"There would be a considerable salary increase—"

"No."

"You're perfect for the job, Kane," Jeff argued. "You know this mill inside and out—"

Kane's hands curled into tight fists on his thighs. He experienced a strange sense of déjà vu and couldn't help but wonder how Megan would feel about him refusing a job promotion and salary increase. He remembered Cathy's bitterness when he'd refused her father's job offer and didn't think he'd be able to stand the same rejection from Megan.

But he couldn't accept the job, either.

He pulled in a deep breath to calm the chaos raging inside him. "Thanks for the offer, but no."

Leaning back in his chair, Jeff regarded Kane speculatively. "Mind if I ask why?"

Kane stared at him, wondering what his boss would say if he told him the truth, that he'd be totally lost in the sea of paperwork the purchasing position required. He remained silent. His gut churned, and a muscle in his jaw ticked.

Jeff released an impatient sigh. "I need to note on your review the reason why you refused the promotion."

"Just put personal reasons."

When had he completely lost control of his life?

Kane scrubbed a hand over his jaw as he drove home from work, an aggravated sound rumbling from his chest. A familiar frustration flooded him, stripping away any bit of confidence he'd been feeling since his conversation with Megan about selling his woodwork. He couldn't even accept a job promotion in an industry he'd been involved in since the age of twelve, and Megan thought he could run his own business?

Pulling into his dirt drive, he swallowed the bitterness rising in his throat. Lately, he'd been feeling as though he was dodging bullets that were increasing in quantity, speed and size. The changes in his life were happening rapidly, and keeping up a pretense required all his concentration. Coping on a day-to-day basis with all the adjustments Megan was making at home was going to push him to the brink of insanity. She was pulling the rug from beneath his feet, constantly making him stumble and grope for balance.

Tired and weary, he got out of the truck, gave Andrew a halfhearted hello and wave as he played in the yard and entered the house through the kitchen. He stopped just inside the threshold, his gaze taking in yet more changes.

She must have unpacked another box of her things and done more shopping in the city. Peach frilly curtains framed the window over the sink, and a floral arrangement sat on the table, along with new matching place mats and cloth napkins at each setting.

He noticed other things, too, new appliances on the counter and dish towels that weren't frayed around the edges. What else had she replaced in the kitchen?

Suddenly feeling irritable and edgy, he set his lunch box on the counter and opened the cupboard where he normally stored packaged and canned foods. Floral patterned plates and bowls had replaced his chipped set of dishes. And the food, he discovered as he rummaged around, was in a different cupboard. Sometime over the past three days she'd gone grocery shopping again and was slowly replacing the brands of food he recognized with her own selections.

He blew out a harsh breath and slammed the cupboard door, which did nothing to calm his escalating temper.

"Kane?"

He spun around and glared at the woman responsible for spinning his world out of control and wreaking havoc with his emotions. The day's accumulation of stress, combined with frantic fears he couldn't name, caused something within him to snap. "I can't find anything in this house anymore! By the time you're done rearranging and decorating everything, will I have anything to call my own?"

Her eyes widened at his outrage and she took a step back, confusion etching her features. He was glad for the distance his anger put between them, but he hated himself for hurting her. Damn, he didn't know what to do or feel anymore.

"I only thought I'd add some of my stuff to the house. If it bothers you..."

Her words faded as his gaze drifted to the stack of banded letters she clutched against her chest. Prickles of apprehension raced down his spine, and his legs turned to jelly. Terror, cold and clammy, gripped him. Oh, God, no...

He started toward her and grabbed the letters, his movements rough enough to startle her. "Where did you get these?" he demanded. But he knew the answer. Knew, too, that she'd discovered more than just these unopened letters. Bile rose into his throat until he thought he might be sick.

Her gaze narrowed, as if she was trying to figure him out and analyze his radical behavior. He didn't like her scrutiny. Not one bit. He deepened his scowl in an attempt to discourage her silent probing.

"I found them in our bedroom," she finally said.

In his closet, buried behind other boxes and old sweaters on the top shelf. Swearing vividly, he charged past her and halted abruptly in the living room, dread squeezing his chest like a vise. The box he'd stashed so carefully in his closet was open, the contents spilling across the coffee table. Unopened letters and correspondence, his parents' marriage and death certificates, a few pictures of his parents and sister, and most telling, Andrew's kindergarten and first-grade workbooks.

The room spun, and he squeezed his eyes closed. Memories rushed in on him, taunting him, forcing him to remember all the nights he'd stayed up late, tracing letters and words in Andrew's workbooks, not knowing what any of it meant.

He felt violated and too damned vulnerable. Like she'd glimpsed the deepest, darkest part of him. Slowly, he turned and looked at her. He trembled, not with rage but with a panic that caused his heart to triple its beat. "What the hell were you doing going through my personal things?"

She moved forward, the first inkling of irritation creasing her brows. "I found the box while I was cleaning."

"You had no right to go through it." He dumped the workbooks into the box, hating them and everything they represented. Everything he'd never have. Like his own cabinetry business. Like a promotion to purchasing that would stimulate his mind more than his boring, monotonous job of unloading logs and guiding them through scaling and cutting machines.

"I have every right." She pulled on his shirt sleeve, hard, until he glowered at her. And wished he hadn't, because there was so much gentleness in her gaze he wanted to purge himself of the humiliating truth. He clenched his jaw. Her irritation and anger he could deal with, but this... Damn, didn't she realize her tenderness had the ability to bring him to his knees?

"Kane, I'm your wife," she said, her voice a shade away from a plea, her eyes the softest shade of blue he'd ever seen. "If you can't trust me, then we don't have much of a marriage."

He pulled his shirt from her grasp, ignoring her and the dull ache throbbing near the vicinity of his heart.

She dragged a shaky hand through her loose hair, then pressed her fingers to her lips, watching as he set the banded letters on the table and gathered his other possessions.

She picked up the stack, and when he tried to take it back, she stepped away, defiantly holding it out of reach. He could have sworn he saw tears shimmering in her eyes, but she blinked, and something hard and determined replaced the moisture.

"These letters are from your sister," she said evenly. "Why haven't you opened and read them?"

Taking the letters from her, he tossed them into the box with the rest of his personal belongings. "It's none of your business."

"Yes, it is my business," she returned heatedly. "No secrets or lies, remember, Kane?"

But he did have a secret, a devastating one, and lies were the only way to keep the truth from driving her away. But wasn't he doing that now?

"Like I said, it's none of your business," he said harshly. He picked up the box and walked away, muttering, "Can't a person have a little privacy?"

He was back to avoiding her.

Sitting on the front porch swing late at night, Megan huddled into the warmth of Kane's sheepskin jacket. Unfortunately, nothing could chase away the chill that had settled deep inside her. Three days had passed since her argument with Kane, three days since he'd touched her or talked to her other than polite, necessary daily conversation.

She stared at the barn, as she'd done the past three nights. A warm glow of light spilled out the door, and occasionally she saw her husband's silhouette pass the window.

His withdrawal hurt, but not as much as the fact that he didn't trust her with certain aspects of his life. Recalling his harsh words about not being able to find anything in his house anymore and not having anything to call his own since she'd added her possessions, she couldn't help but wonder if he was already regretting their marriage and her intrusion into their lives.

Closing her eyes, she swallowed the huge lump lodged in her throat. Was she moving too fast, making too many changes when he wanted to stay in charge? He'd been alone for so many years. She never stopped to think that maybe her direct approach threatened him.

The unopened letters she'd found from his sister and his strong reaction to them and the contents of that box still puzzled her. She thought about the comment Diane had made about Kane never answering any of her letters, yet when she'd confronted Kane with that he'd gotten angry and defensive, then stalked away. And she still had no answers.

Shivering from the cold evening and an aching loneliness that wouldn't go away, Megan leaned her head against the linked chain holding up the swing. She missed the warmth of her husband's arms around her, hated his reserve and politeness when she'd experienced just how tender and giving he could be. He was like a stranger again, cool, distant and unapproachable.

Whatever was wrong with Kane, she wanted to make it better, but he wouldn't let her get close enough to understand his pain or those shadows she occasionally glimpsed in his gaze. Those damned walls of his were up and secured, and she suspected if she went to him or touched him, her efforts would be rejected. As difficult as it was, she had to wait for him to come to her. Like she'd told him, without trust, they had no marriage.

Knowing tonight would be a repeat performance of the past three, with Kane remaining in his workshop until well past midnight when he assumed she was asleep, she sighed and went inside the house. She changed into a pair of old sweats, crawled into bed and snuggled beneath the covers to generate some warmth.

A shiver chased through her body and wrapped around her heart. It was going to be another long, cold, lonely night.

Megan sat in the corner of her and Kane's bedroom where she'd set up her desk and computer for writing. Setting the first draft of her new book aside, she picked up the handmade book Andrew had created out of construction paper, colored markers and his drawings. He'd won first place with his essay book, *Having a Family,* and had proudly presented it to her the night before at his school's open house. Written within the pages, with an abundance of love and care, was a young boy's view of having a family. The only thing the story lacked was a set of smiling grandparents.

She hoped that would change after tonight's dinner with Patricia and Harold. Guilt pricked her conscience. She hadn't told Kane about inviting the Lindens for dinner and had no idea how he'd react. Then again, she had no idea what to expect from him, never knew when something she said or did would set him off like a time bomb.

Sighing, she put Andrew's project on the shelf next to her desk where she could see it every day. After checking on the pot roast, carrots and potatoes slow cooking in the crock pot for dinner, she sat at her desk with a glass of iced tea, ready to immerse herself in her new book and forget about her marriage problems for a few hours.

Around one-thirty she heard Kane enter the house. Her heart raced when his booted steps echoed down the hall and into the bedroom. She didn't turn, though every feminine molecule within her affirmed his presence with a tingling sensation. The mattress springs squeaked as he sat on the edge of the bed behind her, then there were two thumps as he removed his boots.

She closed her eyes as the silence stretched between them. Is this what they had come to? she wondered painfully. Strangers whose only similar interest was Andrew? Dammit, she wanted to end the awful tension. She knew if she didn't say or do something now he'd disappear to his workshop for the afternoon.

She whirled her swivel chair until she faced him. He glanced up, his expression unreadable, his eyes dark and shadowed, concealing his thoughts and emotions. If she reached out she could touch him. If she slid to her knees she'd be kneeling between his strong thighs. She did neither.

"How was work?" Stupid and inane, but other than demanding to know what he was hiding from, she couldn't think of anything witty to say.

He slowly unbuttoned his blue chambray work shirt. "Same as yesterday." His tone was flat and distant.

Manufacturing a smile, she forged on, determined to reach him. "I started a new book. It's called *Andrew's Father Gets Married.*"

The subject of her new book, which paralleled the new event in Andrew's life, didn't so much as cause a flicker of interest from Kane. "That's great."

As emotionless as he was about their conversation, they might as well have been discussing the weather. She wanted to hit him or throw something at him just to rouse some kind of solid emotion.

He shrugged out of his shirt, and her mouth went dry. Liquid desire settled low in her belly, stirring her senses to life.

She dragged her gaze up, meeting his. The heat simmering in the depths stunned her. Her pulse responded with a feathery flutter. "Would you like to read the first draft of my new book?"

A stricken look crossed his features, and his complexion went pale. He'd had the same reaction at the open house when she'd given him Andrew's book to read.

"Kane?" She frowned, trying to understand her husband's shifting moods. "What is it?"

"Nothing," he said, his voice harsh.

He started to stand, but she wasn't about to let him dismiss her so easily. Not this time. With a hand pressed to his chest, she pushed him onto the mattress. Boldly, she straddled his lap and framed his face in her hands, forcing him to confront their problem, and her, head on. He gripped her hips with his hands and attempted to jerk his head away. She held firm. A battle of wills ensued.

"Dammit, Kane, don't lie to me!" *Tell me what's wrong, so I can help make it better.*

His expression hardened.

"I can't take much more of your silence, or the way you're avoiding me." *I miss you. I want you. I ache for you. How can we be so close yet so far apart?*

A shudder racked his body, and his gaze locked on hers in silent communication. *I'm sorry, I never meant to hurt you.*

I know, but whatever's wrong, you can trust me.

Something within him crumbled, filling his eyes with anguish. *I...can't. Oh, God, I can't! I don't want to lose you.*

You won't. Ever. I promise. "I love you," she whispered, the words feeling so perfect. So right.

His lashes drifted closed. "No," he groaned. Shaking his head, he dropped his hands from her hips and gathered her skirt in his fists.

Expecting him to shove her away, she tightened her knees at his waist. "Look at me." The demand came out as a soft invocation.

He did, revealing green eyes stormy with denial. And a need that gave her the strength to lay herself bare. "I love you, Kane. More than I ever thought possible. I won't let you ignore it."

"I don't deserve it." His voice was low and tormented.

"You do. You deserve the love of a good woman, and I'm gonna be the one to give it to you, whether you want it or not."

His body trembled. A flicker of trust brushed his features, the emotion honest and real. As brief as the glimpse was, it was all the sign she needed. She wanted to touch his heart, give him enough love to chase away whatever demons haunted him. Enough love that he'd tell her what caused him so much heartache.

Cradling his head in her hands, she lowered her mouth and sealed her vow with a breath-stealing kiss. His lips parted on a groan, and she slid her tongue past all barriers to tangle and mate with his. He was suffering, and her only thought was to comfort him in the only way she knew he'd accept.

Their mouths fused. His hands gripped her thighs then slid over her hips and waist and along her spine, pulling her so close the only thing separating them was their clothes. She wrapped her arms around his neck, feeling as though she was burning up from the inside out.

She wanted their clothes off and bare skin touching. She wanted him to ease the unbearable ache and loss of being without him. She wanted his love.

Breaking their kiss, she pressed her hands to his chest, feeling the heavy beat of his heart beneath her palms. Staring into eyes hazed with passion, she slowly peeled her camisole top over her head, then unclasped her bra and let both items fall to the floor. Her breasts swelled beneath his hot gaze.

She took his hands and cupped his palms over the firm mounds of flesh. "Make love to me, Kane."

His hands shaped her while his thumbs scraped over her sensitive nipples. "I can't resist you," he said, his voice husky.

"I don't want you to." And to prove it, she pulled him down to the mattress with her, trusting him with her heart and body and hoping the action would prove he could trust her in return.

She loved him. The knowledge filled Kane with a sense of wonder, and doubt, too. He knew how fragile love could be, how easily that illusion of grandeur and happiness could be shattered. Cathy had loved him until she'd learned the truth.

He glanced at the woman snuggled against his chest, napping soundly after a very satisfying afternoon of making love. He cared for Megan, which was more than he'd believed he was capable of giving. No other woman had affected him on such a primitive, emotional level, yet he couldn't bring himself to express his feelings. Fear and insecurities warred with trust.

Gently, he pulled the sheet over her bare shoulder. She sighed and twined her legs around his. Maybe she wouldn't be shocked if he told her the truth, he thought. Maybe she wouldn't reject him. His stomach knotted. It was the flip-side to those maybes, the possibility that she would look at him in disappointment and shame that made him hold back the truth.

God, when had his emotions for Megan become a snarl he couldn't untangle? And why had she gone and complicated things by falling in love with him?

She stirred again, this time lifting her head to look at him. She looked sleepy, disheveled and thoroughly loved. By him. He grinned despite the troubling thoughts plaguing him. If they never had to leave this bedroom and deal with real life, his worries and concerns would be over. Eventually they'd have to get up, but for now he planned to enjoy the quiet, simple moment with his wife.

She propped her chin on the hand resting on his chest. "What are you smiling about?" she murmured.

He touched her flushed cheek, caressed a finger over the swollen lips he'd kissed so ardently. "You."

She smiled, but a regretful sigh escaped her. "We have to get up."

"Why?" he asked lazily.

"For one, Andrew will be home any time."

"And for another?" he asked, wondering how many excuses she had lined up and how he could thwart each one so they could spend the rest of the day in bed.

She hesitated, then released a breath and said, "I invited the Lindens to dinner."

CHAPTER TEN

KANE jerked back and stared at Megan, their warm, intimate aftermath quickly dissolving into chilling reality.

"You did *what?*" His deceptively calm voice belied the fury boiling just beneath the surface.

If his dark scowl concerned her, she didn't show it. "I said, I invited Harold and Patricia to dinner," she repeated easily, as if having his in-laws over for a social gathering was a weekly occurrence instead of a nonexistent event.

"That's what I thought you said." He moved off her, anger giving him a restless kick of adrenaline. He picked up his jeans from the floor and yanked them on.

She sat on the bed, her mussed hair tumbling around her face and shoulders. "Is there a problem with having them over?" Challenge laced her husky voice.

"A problem?" Incredulous laughter escaped him. "We don't get along. We don't like each other. They believe I killed their daughter! I'd call that a *big* problem." He speared his fingers through his hair. "Christ, Megan, what possessed you to do something so stupid?"

He didn't care for the determined tilt to her chin. "I don't think it was stupid. You and your in-laws need to reconcile, and it certainly isn't going to happen when you won't even make the effort to be civil about the situation. Maybe bringing the three of you together will force you to clear the air and settle old grudges."

"Hardly." After Cathy died he'd tried to talk to Patricia, only to have his attempts spurned. Why would five years of separation make any difference? "I can't believe Patricia agreed to this—" he sliced a hand in the air, struggling for an appropriate word "—this *farce.*"

She slid from the bed, slipped on a silky thigh-length

155

robe and fastened the belt. "It'll be a farce only if you make it one," she said dryly.

He narrowed his gaze, keeping a tight focus on the issue at hand. "When were you gonna tell me about this little dinner party you planned?"

Picking up a brush from the dresser, she looked into the mirror and pulled the bristles through the tangles in her hair. "Just before they arrived."

He swore. "How convenient." Moving beside her, he grabbed a T-shirt from a dresser drawer and whipped it over his head. "Nothing like waiting till the last minute to spring your little surprise on me."

She gave an exasperated sigh and tossed the brush down. "Look at you, Kane. This is precisely why I wasn't going to tell you until the last minute. You're getting all worked up for nothing."

"Nothing?" He stood toe to toe with her, his voice rising in fury. "You know what's going to happen when they get here? We're either going to all sit around the living room and glare at one another, or insults and accusations are going to fly fast enough to make your head spin."

"I was hoping we could talk." She jammed her hands on her hips, irritation sparking in her gaze. "You know, maybe try and have a civil, dignified conversation."

"About what? About how miserable I made Cathy? That I was responsible for her death? Great icebreaker, wouldn't you say?" He whirled and paced the floor. "You saw how awkward things were at Andrew's birthday party."

She stepped in front of him, bringing his pacing to an abrupt stop. And then she touched him, gently placing her palm against his cheek. "Give it a chance. Please, Kane."

Clenching his jaw, he grabbed her wrist and pulled her hand away, refusing to give in to the tender emotions weaving around his heart and breaking down his resistance. He'd do anything for Megan, he realized. Anything but this. "No. *Nothing* is going to change the past."

"You're right," she conceded. "But *you* can change the future, if only you'd talk to Harold and Patricia—"

He dropped her hand. "No."

"Fine. If you don't do it for yourself, then do it for Andrew."

Always Andrew. But how could he fault her for caring and loving his son? He couldn't. She was an exceptional mother to Andrew, but he didn't like her meddling in his life. "Andrew has adjusted and will continue to adjust to the situation."

She folded her arms over her chest and scoffed at him. "That's incredibly selfish of you to make *him* adjust when you have the ability to end the tension."

"It's not that simple, Megan." He wished it was. Feeling caged in and edgy, he jammed on his boots, intending to get out of the house and away from Megan and her fallacy of happily ever after.

"You're running again, Kane," she said softly, with a perception that touched a vulnerable part of him.

He glared at her, automatically building a wall between them. It was the only way he knew how to preserve his pride. "Yeah? So what?"

She didn't so much as flinch at his snappish tone. Her gaze held his steadily. "What I want to know is what you're running from."

His heart stopped and resumed at a frantic pace. "You don't want to know."

"That's what you keep telling me, but why don't you let me be the judge of that?"

Because the truth is what destroyed my first marriage. The truth is what stands between me and the Lindens. "The truth will only make matters worse." He headed for the door.

Out of the corner of his eye he saw her step toward him, then stop. "Kane, where are you going?"

One hand on the door handle, he turned, cool mask in place. With effort, he blocked his emotions from the hurt and confusion in her gaze. "I'm going out. If you insist on having this dinner party, you're gonna have to have it without me."

*   *   *

"How come Dad didn't come to church with us today?"

Megan turned her car onto the street heading into town and glanced at Andrew sitting beside her. "He had things to do around the house," she lied. She didn't have the heart to tell him Kane was upset with her. Again.

Andrew frowned, looking doubtful. "Like what?"

"I, uh…" No plausible excuse came to mind, especially when he'd been attending church with Andrew for years. "I think he just wanted some time alone."

Ever since the dinner fiasco he'd been cool and distant, not that his withdrawal was anything new. The man's emotional shields were strong, secure and instinctive. She was beginning to wonder if she stood a chance of permanently breaking them down.

After Kane had stormed out of the house and she'd regained her composure, she'd called Harold to cancel dinner. He'd been understanding but disappointed. He'd spent the past two weeks talking to Patricia about the situation, and although he didn't think his wife was ready to completely forgive and forget the past, he believed in time she might be willing to accept some kind of reconciliation.

"Maybe I shouldn't go to Grandma and Grandpa's today," Andrew said, looking way too serious for an eight-year-old. "I could stay home and we could make Dad some cookies, or maybe a cake."

Megan smiled despite her heavy heart. "Honey, that's a wonderful thought, but your grandparents look forward to their day with you." And she wasn't about to deny the Lindens the pleasure of their grandson. "You know that, don't you?"

"Yeah, but sometimes I wish we could all do stuff together." He hung his head and stared at his lap. "Corey says that his grandma and grandpa come over to his house all the time." He lifted a confused gaze to her. "How come we don't do things like that?"

Because your father is as stubborn as a mule. She sighed, gathering the words to best explain the situation. "Andrew, sometimes families have disagreements. That's what happened with your dad and your grandparents. I'm working on patching things up, but it might take some time."

He smiled, and his dimple appeared. "I knew you would."

She lifted a brow at him as she turned into the church parking lot and searched for a vacant spot. "Knew I would what?"

The self-satisfied look on his face was at once adorable and disarming. "Try and make things better with my dad and Grandma and Grandpa Linden."

Little stinker, she thought affectionately. "You did?"

"Yep. And I think Grandpa likes you."

She knew she had at least one ally with Harold. Turning off the ignition, she asked, "And your grandma?"

He shrugged. "She doesn't say much about you, but that doesn't mean she doesn't like you."

She reached across the console and gently ruffled his hair. "Well, you be sure to tell them both today that I think they're wonderful grandparents."

His eyes sparkled happily. "Okay."

They got out of the car and started toward the church and the crowd of people visiting until the bells tolled. Andrew slipped his hand in hers and looked at her with liquid brown eyes full of worry.

"Do you think Dad's okay at home?"

"I'm sure he's fine." The lie was necessary.

"Will you bake him cookies while I'm at Grandma's?" Hope tinged his voice. "That'll cheer him up for sure."

Megan was desperate enough to try anything to reach Kane. "I'll see what I can do."

Megan wrapped the previous night's leftover fried chicken in foil and placed it in a paper sack along with grapes and the fresh batch of chocolate chip cookies she'd baked when she returned from church. Completing the picnic was the bottle of wine she'd picked up at the grocery store on her way home.

Kane had left for town a little less than an hour ago, saying something about picking up some stuff being held at the hardware store for him. She couldn't have planned this surprise picnic any more perfectly. Knowing he'd be home any moment and wanting to be gone when he did, she quickly wrote a note for him to meet her at the huge oak tree by the lake and signed the note, "I love you, Megan." She placed the piece of paper on the counter by the back door, so he'd be sure to see it when he walked in.

She gathered up her goodies, walked the short trek to their meeting spot and spread out the blanket she'd brought, then unloaded their lunch. When that was done, she reclined on the blanket, unbuttoned the front of her dress to reveal the swells of her breasts, hiked her skirt to her thighs and affected a sultry, seductive pose. And waited.

Kane's cool, distant attitude didn't concern her. She'd decided that she was going to shower him with so much love he'd drown in it, whether he liked it or not. And if seducing him was the only way to shatter his emotional barriers, she'd gladly pay the price.

Seconds stretched into endless minutes as she continued to plan her seductive strategy. The leaves in the trees rustled gently and birds chirped overhead. The sky couldn't have been bluer, the day more beautiful for sharing with someone she loved. Eventually, she succumbed to the cool spring breeze and the gentle lapping of water lulling her to sleep.

She woke from her nap with a start. Drowsily, she looked at her watch. Two hours had passed. Abruptly sitting up, she glanced around, expecting to see Kane. She was alone. Achingly, desperately, frustratingly alone.

Discouraged and stung by his rejection, she packed up the untouched picnic. The walk home seemed like a five-mile uphill climb. The entire way, she told herself there had to be a logical explanation, that most likely Kane had gotten held up in town and hadn't come home yet. Surely he wouldn't intentionally ignore her request?

Her excuses fizzled when she crested the knoll and saw

his truck parked outside the barn. With every step closer to the house, her heart grew heavier. Her fervent vow to shower him with love mocked her. How could she accomplish her goal when Kane wasn't the least bit willing or cooperative?

Angry at herself for believing in the impossible and at Kane for his selfish behavior, she strode into the barn and plunked the sack on his workbench. Kane turned from his current project, eyeing the bag, and her, warily.

The pain inside her grew to startling proportions. "Here's your lunch. It would have been real nice if we could have shared it together, but I guess you weren't in the mood for company, which is nothing new around here." Her words were cruel, but she couldn't stop them.

A startled look resembling guilt passed over his features but was quickly masked by a practiced indifference. "What are you talking about?"

"The note, Kane," she said, her throat raw and her emotions frayed. "The one in the kitchen asking you to meet me by the lake."

He hesitated, then turned away. Taking off his plastic safety glasses, he tossed them aside. "I didn't see any note."

She wanted to scream at him to look at her so she could see the truth in his eyes. "How could you miss it? It's right on the counter as you walk in the kitchen."

Again he paused. Again he wouldn't look at her. "I haven't been up to the house."

She honestly didn't know whether or not to believe him. His answer was sensible, but feeling hurt and emotionally wounded, she held tight to her anger. "Since you only spend time in your workshop, I guess next time I ought to post the note on your workbench!"

He turned. That marble facade of his cracked a bit, giving her a glimpse of vulnerability she wasn't in the frame of mind to dissect or understand. He stepped toward her. "Megan—"

She held up a hand to ward him off, in no disposition to

be rational. "Forget it, Kane. Just forget it." She damned the tears rushing forward and choking her voice. She damned him for breaking her heart when all she wanted to do was love him. She didn't know what to do if he wouldn't at least make an attempt to meet her halfway. "Let's just chalk this up to a misunderstanding, and I won't make the mistake again of expecting anything more from you than what you openly give."

He stood unmoving, looking as miserable as she felt. The thought gave her no pleasure, just filled her with a sadness that went soul deep. He didn't want her heart. He didn't want her love. Who was she to force them on him?

She turned and left the barn before she broke down. As soon as she stepped outside, the sob lodged in her throat escaped and the tears she'd managed to hold at bay spilled over her lashes. The emptiness in her was all-consuming.

She heard him swear, then a loud crash as he threw something against the barn wall. She winced and forced herself to keep walking away. All she wanted to do at the moment was tear that damned note into a million pieces.

Swiping at her wet cheeks, she entered the kitchen and searched the counter for the note, then the floor, then the entire area, nearly turning the kitchen upside down with her urgent need to find that stupid piece of paper.

The note was nowhere to be found.

Megan separated the dirty clothes methodically, her mind numb and her heart battered and bruised. The only time she could remember experiencing such a horrible helplessness and loneliness was after her divorce.

She swallowed the growing knot in her throat, determined not to give in to the urge to cry any more tears than she already had in the past two days. Especially with Andrew in the other room doing his homework.

Biting her bottom lip and blinking back moisture, she grabbed a pair of Andrew's jeans and checked the pockets. She found a gum wrapper, a quarter and a marble before tossing them into the dark clothes pile. She focused her mind on the chore, repeating the process with all his pants, then Kane's, amazed, as always, at the different trinkets and the amount of change she discovered.

Reaching into the front pocket of Kane's jeans, her fingers closed around a crumpled piece of paper and some loose change. She automatically dumped them on her growing pile and dropped the pants on top of the others. It took her mushy brain five seconds to register the significance of that piece of paper, and when it did, everything within her froze.

She stared at the balled up paper as if it were a poisonous insect. Her mind spun and her heart raced so fast she was certain she could hear blood rushing in her ears.

No, it couldn't be. Her stomach rolled. Hands trembling, she forced herself to reach for the paper and smooth out the folds. She held in her hands the note she'd written for Kane three days ago, the same one he'd denied seeing. She moaned, the wounded sound distant to her own ears. But the pain of his betrayal sliced straight to her heart.

Questions flooded her mind faster than she could catalogue them. Why would Kane ignore her note? And why would he lie about finding it? She desperately sought answers, thinking over the past couple of weeks and linking Kane's behavior to each situation that had distanced him more and more. Like a recorded video on fast forward, scenes tumbled through her mind. The panic in his gaze when she'd given him that grocery list, his never having a checking account and paying everything with cash, his insistence on a tutor for Andrew, his insecurities about his woodwork, those unopened letters from his sister....

Like threads in an intricate weaving, every occurrence pulled the interlacing tighter, presenting her with only one logical conclusion.

The truth rippled through her like an electrical shock, and the note slipped from her hand and fluttered to the floor.

"Oh, my God," she breathed.

* * *

Kane knew something was wrong the moment he stepped through the back door into the kitchen and saw Megan sitting so calmly at the kitchen table.

The sight of her red-rimmed eyes, pink nose and pale complexion tipped him off that she'd been crying. Worry gripped him until something crinkled in her hands. His eyes dropped to her lap. Very slowly, very deliberately, she placed a wrinkled piece of paper on the table for him to see.

His gaze shot to hers. She didn't say a word. She didn't have to. Gut instinct told him she *knew*. His body tensed, his barriers going up automatically. He put his lunch box on the counter and retrieved a beer from the refrigerator, taking his time while he waited for accusations to fly.

It had been a mistake to take the note and stuff it in his pocket when he'd found it, but he'd been so frustrated and angry it had been a reflex action. One he regretted. It had been a bigger mistake that he'd forgotten about the note, but guilt had consumed his mind and blocked out all coherent thoughts.

And now he'd pay the price for his stupidity. He wondered if it would cost him his marriage—for the second time. The thought of losing Megan wrenched at his heart. What if she didn't want him after this confrontation was over? And he knew it was coming. Like a brewing storm he could feel the tension, knew it was a matter of time before the fury hit and wiped out everything in its wake. His stomach twisted, and he washed down the bitterness rising in his throat with a long swallow of beer.

He leaned against the counter and looked at her. "Where's Andrew?" he asked, his voice as rough and bristly as he felt.

"Cleaning his room." Her soft voice belied the ruthless intent in her gaze. "I want to know why you lied to me about the note."

A lie sprang to his lips, a natural, involuntary action he'd honed over the years. More lies to cover up an endless string of lies that would never end, just get more difficult to cover up.

He let out a long, hissing breath. "I didn't want to hurt you." But causing her pain was all he'd ever done. He hated himself for that.

"It hurts me that you think you have to hide the truth from me."

Denial was strong and even harder to dismiss when he'd spent a lifetime dodging the truth. "I don't know what you're talking about." Finishing his beer, he tossed the bottle into the container under the sink and headed for the back door.

She came out of her seat and cut him off, her eyes blazing with a fierce and furious light. "Yes, you do, and you're not walking away until this is settled."

He glared at her even as he fought the urge to haul her into his arms, crush her to his chest and never let her go. He was scared, he realized, scared of what the truth would mean to her. Terrified of rejection, and of disappointing the woman who'd come to mean more to him than he had ever dreamed possible.

"What do you want from me?" he asked, his throat clogged with a multitude of emotions.

"I want your trust." *I want your love,* her eyes said. She cupped her hand over his cheek, her gentle touch unraveling something deep within him. "I want to hear the truth, the *real* truth that's tearing us apart, from your lips."

She knew. No matter how he denied the inevitable, it wouldn't go away. And he was so damned tired of bluffing, deceptions and lies. The turmoil of the past months boiled to the surface.

"You want the truth, Megan?" he asked, using anger as a defense. Grabbing her wrist, he pulled her hand away before she could snatch it back when he confessed his darkest secret. "The truth is, I can't read." He steeled himself, waiting for the horrified expression he'd dreaded seeing since the day they married.

Instead, compassion softened her features. "Oh, Kane, why didn't you tell me?"

He dropped her hand and moved away, clawing his fingers through his hair. "What am I supposed to say? Oh, by the way, I can't read, and sorry, honey, I'll never amount to much of anything—"

"Stop it, Kane," she said vehemently.

But he was on a course straight to self-destruction and couldn't stop himself. The frustration and bitterness of a lifetime came rushing forward, and he was helpless to stop any of it. "It's true! I never finished school. Hell, I think the last grade I attended was second, and after my mother died I had to raise my baby sister while my dad worked to support us." The whole story spilled out, how his father insisted his son learn to earn a living, and how grateful Kane had been for his father's misdirected guidance, because he was able to support himself and his sister when his dad died. The sacrifices he'd made had been necessary to survive but had cost him an education.

When it was over, he sank into a chair and hung his head in his hands so he wouldn't have to look at Megan. Christ, what had he done? If he was lucky, she'd just leave him alone in his misery.

Megan wasn't one to give up.

Her warmth and unique feminine scent surrounded him, then her hand touched his back. His muscles jumped and pulled tight. She rubbed lightly, but he wouldn't let go of the tension. It was the only thing holding him together.

"You can learn to read," she said.

His head snapped up, and he scowled at her. "God, Megan, don't you think I've tried that?"

"On your own?" she guessed.

"Yes, and it's nothing but a frustrating, degrading experience."

She sat in the chair next to him, so close their knees nearly touched. "Why haven't you asked anyone for help?"

His laughter lacked humor. "Because I'm not about to

risk the entire town learning I'm illiterate and humiliate myself that way again.''

She frowned. ''Again?''

He nodded jerkily. ''I only told one person about my illiteracy, and I experienced enough humiliation to last me a lifetime.''

''Cathy?''

''Yeah. Not being able to read cost me a job in her daddy's bank, my marriage, and made my wife miserable enough to want a divorce.''

Megan gasped, her gaze widening in astonishment and understanding. ''Oh, my God, that's why you refused the job Harold offered you.''

A bitter smile twisted his lips. ''You can't exactly bluff your way through correspondence, reports and contracts.''

She shook her head, confused. ''But Harold doesn't know you're illiterate.''

''That's because his daughter was too embarrassed and ashamed to let everyone know she married someone stupid,'' he said harshly. ''Thankfully, she took my secret to her grave.''

Anger flashed across Megan's features. ''You're not stupid.''

Restless energy burned through his veins. He bolted out of his seat and across the kitchen, then whirled to face her, hands clenched at his sides. ''I sure as hell feel like it when I can't even read a goddamn note that you leave for me!''

She stood and crossed to him, tears shimmering in her eyes. Eyes that wanted to understand him, help him, love him. If only he'd let her.

Standing in front of him, lip trembling and a single tear escaping, she whispered achingly, ''It doesn't have to be this way.''

His jaw hardened. ''Dammit, Megan, I don't want your pity!''

''I'm not crying because I pity you, you big lug,'' she said, grabbing a handful of his shirt and giving him a furious shake. ''I hurt for you.''

He didn't touch her, but lord, he wanted to. He wanted to sink his fingers into her silky hair, kiss her lips and wake from this horrible nightmare with her arms around him. But this was living reality, and he wasn't worth those tears welling in her eyes and trickling over her lashes.

He looked away, anywhere but in those velvet blue eyes that reached into his heart and soul and tugged like nothing he'd ever experienced. He couldn't respond for the lump in his throat.

"I came into this marriage with very few expectations, Kane," she said, her voice soft with regret. "I wanted to be a mother for Andrew and I wanted to be your wife. Along the way, I hoped we could come to mean something special to one another. I'd hoped we could share secrets, hopes and fears. I love you, Kane. Doesn't that mean anything to you?"

It meant everything to him. Everything he'd ever hoped for and dreamed of but thought he was destined to live his life without. Hadn't he learned that love wasn't always enough?

"This doesn't have to be the end, Kane," she implored. "If you let it, it can be a new beginning."

"This is the way it is." His tone was as gravelly as sandpaper, his heart and mind confused.

"Fine."

With sickening dread and a withering feeling, Kane watched Megan slip the ring from her left hand and place the gold wedding band on the wrinkled note still on the table. The note he couldn't read.

She held her head determinedly, but her chin trembled. "When you're ready to face your illiteracy, and you're ready to trust me, then we can have a real marriage and be a real family."

This time, it was Megan who walked away.

CHAPTER ELEVEN

"DAD, what does illiterate mean?"

Kane lowered the forkful of scrambled eggs midway to his mouth, grateful that Megan was taking a shower. A slow burning sensation crept from the collar of his work shirt and over his face.

"Why do you want to know?" He winced. Damn, he hadn't meant to sound so gruff.

Frowning, Andrew pushed his eggs around on his plate. "'Cause I heard you and Mom fighting because you're..." He scrunched up his nose, concentrating. "Illiterate."

Kane squirmed in his seat, chagrined and uneasy that his son had overheard their argument and that he was about to learn his father couldn't read. He wasn't about to lie to Andrew. There had already been too many deceptions that had torn this household apart.

"I don't like it when you guys fight, Dad," Andrew said before Kane could answer his first question, giving him a brief reprieve.

"I don't like it, either." Having Megan emotionally shut him out for the past three days bothered him more than he cared to admit. The irony of their situation struck him, because now he knew exactly how he'd made her feel all those times he'd pushed her away. Isolated. Lonely. Empty. After he had experienced how warm, open and giving his wife could be, her withdrawal was killing him.

He carried her wedding band in his pocket, and there wasn't an hour that ticked by that he didn't think about what she'd said or recall how devastated he'd felt when she'd removed the ring. Except he feared he lacked the finesse to patch things up. He feared it was too late for apologies.

He briefly squeezed his eyes shut to ward off the throbbing in his temples. Somehow, he knew an apology wasn't what Megan was looking for.

"I think Mom feels bad." Andrew picked at the crumbs on his piece of toast, giving the task more attention than it warranted. "She doesn't smile half as much anymore, and she always looks like she's been crying."

Kane swallowed a gulp of hot coffee, trying to save himself from responding to *that* observation. What was he supposed to say? "Yeah, son, I'm the one making Megan miserable. I'm the one with more pride than sense." He inwardly groaned at the truth of that statement.

Even though Megan had pried his deepest, darkest secret from him, not once did she ridicule him, nor had she rejected him, even when he wanted her to so he wouldn't have to face his own failures, his own shame. The woman was incredible, unwavering in her support even as she walked away from him. *When you're ready to face your illiteracy, and you're ready to trust me, then we can have a real marriage and be a real family.*

She'd put the ball in his court, and he was floundering, grappling to find just the perfect backhand to return the serve. He was scared of screwing up, but most of all, he feared losing Megan.

"So what does that big word mean, Dad?"

They were back to his illiteracy. Drawing a deep breath, he said, "It means I can't read." He held what little breath was left in his lungs, waiting for his son to burst out laughing, tease him or slink away in embarrassment.

Andrew looked at his father thoughtfully. "Oh," he said, then brightened marginally. "I could teach you to read."

His son's unconditional acceptance relieved him. "I'll think about that."

Andrew's support, combined with Megan's, should have given him enough self-confidence to tackle the world. Yet he couldn't stop the doubts and the memories of another woman's rejection.

Megan was nothing like his first wife, his conscience argued. From the moment he'd met her she'd been nothing but giving and understanding, believing in him even though he gave her no reason to.

"I hope you guys make up real soon," Andrew said, bringing Kane back to their conversation. "I want to see her smile and laugh again. And you, too, Dad." Tears filled his eyes. "I don't want you and Megan to be like how it is between you and Grandpa and Grandma Linden."

Aw, hell. Lately, it seemed he'd caused the people in his life nothing but heartache and tears. Megan was right. He *was* selfish, thinking only of himself and not the needs of his family. He'd used his illiteracy as an excuse not to confront his past, he realized. He'd kept the rift between him and the Lindens fueled by keeping the truth buried beneath layers of resentment.

The school bus horn blared, and Andrew slid out of his seat, mumbled a goodbye to Kane and pushed out the back door. Kane let him go, unwilling to make his son promises he didn't know if he could keep.

Sighing deeply, he cleared their dishes from the table, thinking about the woman who'd become his wife. A woman who'd *wanted* to be his wife. He hadn't realized how empty and lonely he'd been until he met Megan, hadn't known a woman's love could be so good.

He loved her. There was no sense denying the warm, fuzzy emotion wrapped around his heart. And if he loved her, didn't he owe it to her to do whatever it took to make their marriage work? To shelve his pride for her and give her the trust she'd worked so hard to earn?

His first marriage had ended tragically, and he couldn't change that. But he had the ability to try to make amends with the Lindens and start fresh, not only for Andrew's sake, but for the sake of his new marriage.

Because, ultimately, he wasn't willing to risk losing the best thing that had ever happened to him and his son.

He'd been acting strange all morning.

Megan stole a sideways glance at Kane as they pulled out of Jeff and Karen's driveway after dropping Andrew off to spend the night. She'd learned from Karen that Kane had made arrangements to pick Andrew up tomorrow, after they attended church services.

That left her alone with Kane for a good twenty-four hours.

Under normal circumstances she would have thoroughly enjoyed a day and night with her husband all to herself. But it wasn't as if they were experiencing wedded bliss at the moment, the kind where you couldn't keep your hands off each other and you spent every waking hour thinking of ways to be with the one you loved. No, their marriage had become one of convenience, and she hated it.

He hadn't said two words to her since this morning, when he'd told her they were going out that afternoon. She had no idea where out was, and by the look of concentration on Kane's face and his white-knuckled grip on the steering wheel as he drove through town, it wasn't somewhere fun, exciting or romantic.

"Do you plan on telling me where we're going?" she asked.

He never took his gaze off the road. "You'll see when we get there."

She sat back in her seat, stared out the passenger window and waited until Kane finally braked to a stop in front of the Lindens' house.

She glanced from the two-story structure to Kane, feeling curious as well as cautious. He turned off the ignition, removed the key and took a deep breath that did nothing to ease the tight lines around his mouth and eyes.

"What are we doing here?" she asked quietly.

He met her gaze, and the vulnerability in the depths touched a tender chord in her. "I think it's past time we all had a dignified conversation, don't you?"

Hope swelled in her heart. "You already know how I feel about that."

A crooked smile claimed his lips. "I guess I'm taking you up on your advice. Ready?"

She glanced at the house, wondering how the Lindens

were going to react to this impromptu visit. "Are you sure you want me to go with you?"

Sincerity darkened his eyes. "I can't do this without you by my side. You give me an incredible amount of courage." He opened his door, but before he could slide out, she grabbed his arm. He looked at her. "What's wrong?"

"Nothing's wrong." She dampened her bottom lip with her tongue. "I think what you're about to do is important, for so many reasons, but…"

"Yes?" He frowned, emphasizing his sudden apprehension.

"Kane, I need to know, are you doing this for me?"

He reached out and gently brushed his knuckles across her cheek in a feather caress. His eyes glowed with a deep, abiding emotion she'd never seen before. "No, I'm doing it for *me,* so I can put the past to rest. And for us, so we can be a family."

The heaviness weighing on her heart the past week lifted. No matter what happened here today, she knew they were going to make it together. Kane's unselfish gesture was proof that he cared enough to make their marriage work.

She followed him up the walkway. After he rang the doorbell, she slid her hand into his, giving him whatever support she could, even if it was a physical connection of warmth and love. He stared at the door as if it were a portal into his past and he wanted no part of it. His palm was damp against hers, and he shifted anxiously as they waited.

"Are you nervous?" Stupid question, but she wanted to keep him talking so he didn't freeze up when the door opened.

"A little," he admitted, then added wryly, "I'm fully expecting Patricia to slam the door in my face."

Luckily, Harold answered the door, looking at first startled, then concerned. "Is Andrew okay?"

When Kane just stared without answering, Megan said, "Andrew's fine." *Come on, Kane, don't back out on me now!*

"Who is it, dear?" Patricia's voice drifted from behind

Harold, then she appeared next to her husband in the entryway. Her eyes widened when she saw who her guests were. The only word she managed to utter was a surprised, "Oh!"

Kane retreated a small step, and Megan tightened her grip on his hand. She felt him take a deep breath, then he said on a rush of expelled air, "Patricia, can we come in? We…I'd like to talk to you and Harold."

Patricia fingered the string of pearls around her neck, her mouth pursing. "Whatever you have to say, you can say it from where you are."

Megan's gaze shot to Harold, silently imploring his assistance before they lost what little ground they'd gained.

"Give the man a chance, Patty," Harold said hastily. "Come on in, both of you." Grabbing his wife firmly by the arm, he led them all into the living room.

They sat opposite each other on the couch and matching love seat. Patricia shifted uncomfortably on the sofa cushion, Kane rubbed his palms down his jeans-clad thighs, and Harold gave Megan a helpless look that said, *Now what are we supposed to do?*

Awkward was a generous description for the tension filling the room. She prompted Kane with a gentle nudge to his side.

He cleared his throat and stopped the nervous motion of his hands by clenching his fingers into his thighs. "There's…" His voice cracked and he cleared it again. "There's something I need to tell the both of you," he said in a steady, determined tone. "Something I should have told you a long time ago. I…I'm illiterate."

There was a moment of silence as Harold and Patricia stared in disbelief.

"Good God!" Harold said, looking more miffed than appalled by Kane's declaration.

A horrified expression transformed Patricia's expression. "You can't read?"

Megan winced at her high-pitched, condescending tone and fought the urge to jump up and defend her husband.

"No, I can't," Kane replied calmly.

Patricia's hand fluttered to her pearls. "You can't be serious!"

"I'm very serious." He took a deep breath, as if to build up more fortitude to continue. "It's the reason I had to refuse the job Harold offered me at the bank."

Patricia gasped. "But...but Cathy never told us!"

"She led us to believe you flat-out refused the job because you didn't want to accept any handouts. It was never a handout, Kane."

"I know." Kane's mouth stretched into a grim line. "Cathy didn't tell you the truth because she was humiliated that I couldn't read and had to refuse the job. She didn't want anyone to know I was illiterate, and I was too embarrassed to say anything."

Harold cocked his head curiously. "So why are you telling us this now?"

Kane looked at Megan, and she gave him an encouraging smile that she hoped conveyed all the love in her heart.

He met his in-laws' gazes. "Because I was hoping we could bury the hatchet and start over with a clean slate."

"Don't you think you're five years too late?" Patricia stood, tears brimming in her eyes. "This hardly brings Cathy back!"

"I'm sorry about Cathy," Kane said with quiet compassion. "But I'm not responsible for her death. I loved her while we were married, but she's gone, and nothing any of us say or do will change what has happened."

"Cathy was all we had!" The accusation escaped on a watery sob of despair and maternal anguish.

"I know." Kane hung his head for a moment, hands clasped between spread thighs, then raised his gaze to Patricia's. "All we have left of Cathy is Andrew, and I know he loves all of us. Can we try and be friends, or at least be civil with one another, for his sake?"

Harold grabbed his wife's trembling hand and gently tugged her to the sofa beside him. "I think we should try," he said to his wife.

"I do, too," Megan echoed.

Patricia broke down, clinging to her husband for comfort. "I love that little boy more than anything!"

"Then let the resentment go, Patricia," Megan said. "There's no reason we can't be a family together."

"Family?" Patricia's voice cracked with uncertainty.

"Yes, a family," Kane said, securing his hand within Megan's. "Megan is my wife, and she's a part of Andrew's life now, too. We come as a complete package."

"We'll take it," Harold said before his wife could issue any objections. "This rift has gone on too long. It's time that it ends, here and now."

Much to everyone's surprise, Patricia gave a shaky nod and whispered, "Yes, it'll end here."

As soon as they entered the living room at home, Megan turned and wrapped her arms around her husband's neck, positive the love and adoration she felt for him was reflected in her eyes. "I'm *very* proud of you."

His hands swept down her spine, molding her body to his. His gaze was clear, free of the emotional barriers that had kept them separated for so long. "Yeah?"

She nodded, threading her fingers through the soft hair at the nape of his neck. "You were wonderful."

"How wonderful?" he asked, his darkening gaze zeroing in on her mouth.

She liked this new, unreserved Kane. "Wonderful enough to make me want to kiss you."

"Yeah?" he asked huskily.

She smiled, welcoming the warm, melting sensation pooling low in her belly. "Yeah."

"Go ahead," he murmured, lashes falling to half-mast. "Show me how wonderful I was."

He was a scoundrel, but she loved him, and she certainly couldn't refuse his request. She drew his head down, and their lips met and parted on twin sighs. The silken slide of his tongue against hers sent a shiver coursing down her spine, ending where his hands linked and held her to him.

There was an awesome tenderness to the kiss, a special spark that transcended everything they'd shared before this day. No longer did she taste a loneliness that made her ache, and the need she sensed was of a different variety— more intimate and less urgent, as if they had the rest of their lives to satisfy every craving they had for one another.

He lifted his mouth from hers, but she didn't mind, because she knew there would always be more, anytime she wanted it. She slid her hands down until they pressed against the strength of his chest. The wild heartbeat beneath her palms matched the staccato rhythm of hers.

He rested his forehead against hers, both of them breathless but in no hurry to rush the inevitable when they had the rest of the day and night alone.

"There's something very important I want to ask you," he said.

"Anything."

He chuckled, his grin a combination of wickedness and sin. "I'll hold you to that later, sweetheart, but for now…I want to know if you'll help me learn to read."

His hesitant request touched her. "I would have been hurt if you hadn't asked me."

Relief relaxed his features. He pulled back to look in her eyes but didn't let go of her. If anything, his hold tightened. "There's so much I want to do, so much I've missed as a result of being illiterate. I want to experience it all. With you."

"I'd like that. Very much." She smiled, tilting her head. "You know, there's something I've been wondering."

"What's that?"

"How do you manage everyday life without being able to read?" She felt her cheeks flush at her personal question, but Kane didn't seem to mind. "I mean, everywhere you look there's something that requires reading of some sort."

"You rely on other talents." He shrugged, not knowing any other way to deal with his handicap. "I'm not exactly proud of how I've gotten by, but you learn where your limitations are and stay within them. You recognize labels, signs, packaging, that sort of thing.''

She found that aspect of his life fascinating, but knew something better lay ahead for him. ''You won't have to do that any longer.''

''Mm.'' He claimed her lips and kissed her again. When he finally lifted his head, a pleasant buzz shimmered through her body.

''There's something else I forgot to tell you,'' he said, nuzzling the sensitive spot just below her ear.

She automatically tensed, thinking he had more secrets he hadn't shared with her. ''There's more?'' she asked cautiously.

''Yeah, lots more.'' His lips skimmed her throat, and his hands began to roam. ''Lots of love,'' he murmured.

Cupping his face in her hands, she made him look at her. Striking green eyes shone with desire and a more powerful emotion that stole her breath.

''What are you saying, Kane?'' she whispered, afraid to put too much stock in his words or that wonderfully cherishing look in his gaze.

''That I love you, Megan Fielding,'' he said, as if she should have known.

Her heart soared, and tears of joy filled her eyes. ''Oh, Kane, I love you, too.''

''Oh, and there's more.''

This time she wasn't worried. Releasing her, he dug into the front pocket of his jeans and withdrew a ring—not her wedding band, but a new band encircled with glittering diamonds.

The elegant, extravagant gift astonished her. Peeling her gaze from the ring, she looked at Kane. ''It's absolutely beautiful, but you didn't have to, I mean, it must have cost a small fortune, and I don't need anything fancy. Your mother's simple gold wedding band is just fine—''

''I wanted you to have it,'' he said, cutting off her babbling. ''And you're worth every penny. To hell with being practical.''

Practical? She raised a brow. "Am I missing something here?"

"I told myself that I married you for practical reasons, but our marriage has been anything but practical."

"Or predictable."

"Especially predictable." He grinned, but his gaze was soft with the love he'd professed. "Practical bit the dust the moment I realized I love you. Now we're partners."

"I like the sound of that."

He picked up her left hand and slid the ring onto her ring finger, making her his wife once again. "The woman at the jewelry store told me they call it an eternity band. And since you're stuck with me for eternity, I thought it was appropriate."

"Very appropriate." She laughed and threw her arms around him for a hug as warm as sunshine, and a soul-deep kiss that wrapped around their hearts.

They came up for air, and Kane gazed at her reverently. "Ah, Megan, I didn't realize how lonely and empty I was until you came into my life. I love you and I need you," he said, his voice rough with passion. "But right now, at this moment, I *want* you."

She gave him a sultry, upswept glance full of sass and desire. "How much do you want me?"

"More than my next breath."

And then she stole his breath with a kiss that promised an eternity of love and laughter and tender, special memories.

Andrew could hardly believe his eyes. His mom and dad were talking to Grandma and Grandpa Linden. And they were all smiling!

The church bells tolled, announcing the beginning of Sunday service. Everyone started filtering into the white building. Megan turned, her gaze scanning the yard. When she found him playing with Corey and Tanner, she smiled and waved at him to come join the family.

He skipped toward them, joy nearly filling him to bursting. He had a family! It had taken some time, and his father had been very stubborn at first about Megan, but he'd known his dad would eventually fall in love with her. How could he not?

He slipped his hand into Megan's and beamed at her. He had a mom he loved. His dad had a wife who made him laugh and smile a lot. At night, when they thought he was sleeping, he heard their soft laughter and whispered words drifting from the living room. And his grandma and grandpa weren't angry with his dad anymore.

He'd found the perfect woman for all of them.

Now, there was only one thing left to do. He glanced at Megan and blurted, "When can I have a brother or sister?"

His mom blushed and his dad chuckled. Delight sparkled in Grandpa's eyes, and a smile touched Grandma's mouth.

His mom and dad exchanged that special look he'd seen them share before, then his dad ruffled his hair. "We'll get to work on it, son," he promised.

Andrew grinned. He could hardly wait for the stork to arrive.

EPILOGUE

"ANDY Gets a New Sister." Kane read the title of Megan's new book out loud to his audience of two. The words were slow and precise, but his voice was strong, clear and steady. He flipped open the book and showed the bright, colorful illustrations to the two kids sitting on either side of him before beginning the story about Andy's newest adventure.

Megan leaned against the door frame to Andrew's room and smiled at the cozy scene within, a content feeling adding to the love she harbored for her family. She'd received her advance copy of *Andy Gets a New Sister* that afternoon and was pleased with the book and the illustrations that depicted Andrew and his two-and-a-half-year-old sister, Emily.

While Kane read the story, Andrew interjected comments, explaining to his little sister about the exciting adventures Andy got himself into, and that when she got older, he'd show her his entire collection of books. And maybe he'd take her on an adventure all their own so their mother could write about it.

Emily, with her big blue eyes and silky raven hair, alternately stared in awe at her big brother, then Kane, clutching the teddy bear Andrew had given her the day she'd been born.

They were outgrowing their little house. Andrew shared his room with Emily, but they'd decided to expand another two rooms, one for Andrew and one for her office. She was quickly outgrowing her small corner in the bedroom and needed her own space, especially now that she'd received approval from her editor to start another children's series, this one entitled *Emily's Escapades.*

Life was good. The past three years had been a lot of hard work, filled with frustrating moments and arguments—Kane could be so stubborn!—but the love her family shared and the close bond they'd established more than made up for any hardship.

Kane read the last page, then closed the book and looked up, meeting her gaze. He gave her a private smile that still had the ability to make her feel sparks of excitement and anticipation, then he stood, his focus on the kids.

"Okay, kiddos, time for bed," he said. "We've got church tomorrow."

Andrew bounced off Emily's bed and into his own. Megan kissed him and wished him sweet dreams while Kane did the same to Emily, then they switched children.

Megan tucked the covers around Emily and kissed her brow.

"See Gama and Poppa Linden 'marrow, Mama?" Emily asked brightly.

Megan smiled. "Yes, sweetie, you'll see Grandma and Grandpa Linden tomorrow after church."

The Lindens had adopted Emily as another grandchild. Not only did Andrew and Emily spend Sundays with their grandparents, the Lindens dropped by regularly to visit. It had taken some time for Patricia to become comfortable with the family thing, but Megan had gone out of her way to make her welcome in their home. Her patience and persistence had paid off. Now, a couple times a week Patricia "found herself in the area" and dropped in to say hello. Megan saw through the woman's ploy and thought it quite cute the way she made excuses for her visits. Funny how she always had a little something with her for the kids.

"'Night," Megan said, and received two sleepy replies. She snapped off the light and closed the door halfway. She headed toward the living room, but as she passed Kane he snagged her hand and pulled her in the opposite direction...toward their bedroom. She didn't protest.

"Emily's growing so fast," Megan said from the middle of the bedroom.

"And she's just as beautiful as her mother." He locked their door with a soft click and gave her a sexy smile that made her bare toes curl. Slowly, he approached her, and her heart raced at the predatory gleam in his eyes.

"Ready for another one?" he asked as his fingers deftly unbuttoned her blouse, revealing a champagne-colored satin bra and more satin skin. His mouth glanced off her shoulder as he pushed the garment down her arms to pool on the floor.

She gasped and let her head fall back so he could taste more of her. "Maybe one more," she managed. "Once your shop gets established."

Kane had finally succumbed to her urging to do what he loved. Learning to read had given him the confidence to reach for his dreams. With Harold's help he acquired a business loan from the bank, then opened a small shop in town for cabinetry. So far, business had been steady. Twice a week in the evenings Kane attended adult education classes and planned to eventually get his high school diploma.

"Mmm." It was Kane's only response. He nibbled the tender flesh of her neck, little love bites that coaxed a series of shivers from her. "Mrs. Scheibe came in and ordered a custom-made hope chest for her daughter, and Billy Telman wants me to help him build a workbench and cupboards in his garage."

She fisted his hair in her hands and gently pulled his head back until he was looking at her. She feigned a pout. "When are you going to find time for me?"

"I *always* find time for you." His reply was a low, sexy growl.

She smiled and skimmed the hem of his shirt up and over his head, then reached for the buckle on his jeans. In less than ten seconds they lay in a heap on the floor, leaving him completely, gloriously naked.

"How about a lesson tonight?" she asked. The question had become their code for making love, because those late-night lessons had inevitably ended up with them in bed discovering other pleasures.

He laughed throatily, then groaned as her fingers played along his belly. "Spelling test tonight?"

She nipped at his chin. "We haven't had one in a while, have we?" She'd invented an enjoyable, amusing game for Kane to learn to spell—by spelling body parts and having him identify them, then giving him a body part and having him spell it. He'd been a quick learner and a very willing pupil. Three years ago it had been hard work, now it was just plain fun.

"Nope. I've missed them." He shimmied her jeans and panties down her legs and off, then skimmed his palms up her calves to her thigh. Squeezing gently, he spelled it.

"Very good," she said on a catch of breath. Those hands of his were incredible. He unsnapped her bra, her last article of clothing, and dropped it on the pile on the floor. He palmed the full weight, and her nipples peaked into aching buds.

"Breast," he murmured, and spelled it, then lowered his mouth to swirl his tongue around the tip.

She moaned, reveling in the exquisite sensations rippling through her. "Very, *very* good," she managed to say before she lost the ability to think beyond what he was doing to her.

He kissed her then, deep and wild and drugging. Walking her backward to the bed, he followed her onto the soft comforter, his hard, muscular body pressing into soft, feminine curves. Automatically, she made room for him, waiting for that first thrust that irrevocably made her unravel into a million different pieces.

But instead of taking her, he braced on his elbows on either side of her and gently smoothed wispy strands of hair from her face. Her lashes fluttered open, and she gazed at him curiously.

His eyes turned a smoky green color, brimming with emotion. "I-L-U-V-U," he spelled.

A crooked smile tipped her mouth. "I think we need to practice that one a bit more," she whispered.

"That's what I was hoping you'd say." He grinned

wickedly, leaving no doubt in Megan's mind that his spelling error was a ploy to steal her heart and soul for the millionth time. "Why don't I just *show* you how much I love you...."

In 1999 in Harlequin Romance® marriage is top of the agenda!

Get ready for a great new series by some of our most popular authors, bringing romance to the workplace! This series features gorgeous heroes and lively heroines who discover that mixing business with pleasure can lead to anything...even matrimony!

Books in this series are:

January 1999
Agenda: Attraction! by Jessica Steele

February 1999
Boardroom Proposal by Margaret Way

March 1999
Temporary Engagement by Jessica Hart

April 1999
Beauty and the Boss by Lucy Gordon

May 1999
The Boss and the Baby by Leigh Michaels

From boardroom...to bride and groom!

Available wherever Harlequin books are sold.

HARLEQUIN®
Makes any time special ™

HRMTB

MEN at WORK

All work and no play?
Not these men!

October 1998
SOUND OF SUMMER by Annette Broadrick

Secret agent Adam Conroy's seductive gaze
could hypnotize a woman's heart. But it was
Selena Stanford's body that needed saving—
when she stumbled into the middle of an
espionage ring and forced Adam out of
hiding....

November 1998
GLASS HOUSES by Anne Stuart

Billionaire Michael Dubrovnik never lost a
negotiation—until Laura de Kelsey Winston
changed the boardroom rules. He might
acquire her business...but a kiss would cost
him his heart....

December 1998
FIT TO BE TIED by Joan Johnston

Matthew Benson had a way with words
and women—but he refused to be tied
down. Could Jennifer Smith get him to
retract his scathing review of her art by
trying another tactic: tying him *up?*

Available at your favorite retail outlet!

MEN AT WORK™

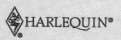 

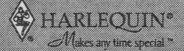

Looking For More Romance?

Visit Romance.net

Check in daily for these and other exciting features:

Hot off the press

View all current titles, and purchase them on-line.

What do the stars have in store for you?

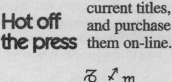

Horoscope

Hot deals

Exclusive offers available only at Romance.net

Plus, don't miss our interactive quizzes, contests and bonus gifts.

PWEB

ℋarlequin Romance®

Coming Next Month

In January look out for a brand-new trilogy featuring the cutest cowboys in the whole state of Texas:

#3535 HAND-PICKED HUSBAND Heather MacAllister

The whole state of Texas seems convinced that Autumn Reese was born to be Clayton Barnett's bride. The whole state bar Clay and Autumn, that is. Which is why she and Clay have dared each other to sign up at the Yellow Rose Matchmakers. Only, watching Clay date other women has made Autumn realize that perhaps her Mr. Right might just be the one she's had within her grasp all along....

Texas Grooms Wanted! is a brand-new trilogy in Harlequin Romance®. Meet three heroines who are all looking for very special Texas men—their future husbands!

Texas Grooms Wanted!: *Only cowboys need apply!*

Also starting in January, find out what happens after office hours in:

#3536 AGENDA: ATTRACTION! Jessica Steele

Edney had been grateful when a handsome stranger had saved her from the unwanted attentions of another man—and amazed when that stranger had kissed her and asked her out to dinner! But Saville Craythorne was not amused. He'd discovered that his new PA was the girl he'd rescued—and he *never* mixed business with pleasure!

Marrying the Boss—*When marriage is top of the agenda!*

#3537 ONLY BY CHANCE Betty Neels

Henrietta's life hadn't been easy. Then, with the help of consultant neurosurgeon Mr. Adam Ross-Pitt, her small world changed irrevocably. He was, of course, far beyond her reach, and if her gratitude to him tipped into love, there was no need for him to know—even if he did keep coming to her rescue!

#3538 MAKE-BELIEVE MOTHER Pamela Bauer and Judy Kaye

Bryan Shepard wanted a mother, and new neighbor Alexis Gordon was perfect for the job. He just had to convince his dad she'd make the perfect wife....

Kids & Kisses—*Where kids and kisses go hand in hand!*